Richard Dalgety grew up in the UK and graduated from Nottingham University. He has spent the last eighteen years working as an international charity fundraiser, fundraising manager and global fundraising specialist. He has worked for organisations like Shelter, Oxfam International, SOS Children's Villages International, UNICEF, Smile Train, Cancer Research UK, Action Aid, Save the Children, Amnesty International, Friends of the Earth, Help the Aged International, The Children's Society, Action Medical Research, Care International, Scope, Rethink, NSPCC, Barnardo's, The Leprosy Mission, Children International and The Nature Conservancy. *Fifth Season* is his fourth collection of short stories/poetry.

Also by the author

I Wasn't Made for These Times – 2004
I'm Not Like Everybody Else – 2017
If I Ever Get Out of This World Alive – 2021

Fifth Season

*A collection of poems and short stories
to give hope in desperate times.*

Richard Dalgety

Copyright © 2022 Richard Dalgety

The moral right of the author has been asserted.

Apart from any fair dealing for the purposes of research or private study, or criticism or review, as permitted under the Copyright, Designs and Patents Act 1988, this publication may only be reproduced, stored or transmitted, in any form or by any means, with the prior permission in writing of the publishers, or in the case of reprographic reproduction in accordance with the terms of licences issued by the Copyright Licensing Agency. Enquiries concerning reproduction outside those terms should be sent to the publishers.

This is a work of fiction. Names, characters, businesses, places, events and incidents are either the products of the author's imagination or used in a fictitious manner. Any resemblance to actual persons, living or dead, or actual events is purely coincidental.

Matador
Unit E2 Airfield Business Park,
Harrison Road, Market Harborough
Leicestershire. LE16 7UL
Tel: 0116 279 2299
Email: books@troubador.co.uk
Web: www.troubador.co.uk/matador
Twitter: @matadorbooks

ISBN 978 1803133 140

British Library Cataloguing in Publication Data.
A catalogue record for this book is available from the British Library.

Printed and bound in the UK by TJ Books Limited, Padstow, Cornwall
Typeset in 11pt Minion Pro by Troubador Publishing Ltd, Leicester, UK

Matador is an imprint of Troubador Publishing Ltd

'If you're always trying to be normal, you will never know how amazing you can be'

Maya Angelou

'Impossible is just a big word thrown around by small men who find it easier to live in the world they've been given, than to explore the power they have to change it. Impossible is not a fact. It's an opinion. Impossible is not a declaration. It's a dare. Impossible is potential. Impossible is temporary. Impossible is nothing'

Muhammad Ali

Contents

Poems

This Train Is Bound for Glory	1
One Day or Day One	2
The Red Sky	3
Fifth Season	4
Tucson, Arizona	5
Vienna Stadtpark	6
September	7
It Doesn't Matter Anymore	8
Russian Roulette	9
Create Something Today	10
Goodbye Blue Monday	11
Planted Planted Planted	12
My Bulletproof Friend	13
My City Is a Question Mark	14
Positive Street	16
Still Snowing in Bergen	17
Cobwebs of Your Mind	19
Salford Snowfall	21
The Comeback Kid	23
Boats to Build	24
Ocean Beach	25
Collette	26
The Quiet One	27
That Subverted Bayeux Tapestry	28
Boys and Girls in Manchester	30
Mr Clean	31
Refuse to Bend	32

Living in New York City	33
Cobwebs and Strange Spiders	35
My Wartime Jacket	36
Lord Byron	37
A Fierce Friend	38
Never Gonna Retire	39
This One Is Optimistic	40
Sex Beats the Devil	41
2022	43
Downstream	44
You Can Hear the Bombers Overhead	45
Bacchanalia	46
Whiskey Man	47
Alana, the Gangster's Beautiful Daughter	48
Set the House Ablaze	50
A Collector	51
37 Miracles	52
Consistency	53
Time Is Tight	54
San Francisco Nights	55
Sourdough Mountain	56
New York City Poem Number Five	57
Dear Young Writers Quarterly	58
Tomorrow Is a Long Time Away	59
This House Is Rocking	60
Salford, North-West England, February 2022	61
Lone Star State Girl	63
Plodding Wins the Race	64

Short Stories

Like a Butterfly at Night	65
New Year's Eve	69

Wild Billy's Circus Story	76
Not to Be Taken Away	78
Hunting Dean Moriarty in Manchester	85
Two of Us	93
Everybody's Happy Nowadays	101
Please, Please, Please, Let Me Get What I Want	107
Prospect Heights	112
Blackpool Girl	127

This Train Is Bound for Glory

I am not scared of the world anymore
I have decided to come out of hibernation
You tell me to eat lima beans
I will eat lima beans
You tell me to order an acai fruit bowl
I will eat an acai fruit bowl
You tell me to dose up on antibiotics and apple cider vinegar
I will dose up on antibiotics and apple cider vinegar
You tell me to focus on avocados, blueberries and macadamia nuts
Bell peppers, brown rice, dark chocolate
Ezekiel bread and extra virgin olive oil
You got it

Whilst you are at work
I might even get myself a Ronnie Wood haircut
I have got my own book to write
Spray-paint the shadows in the gloaming
Start all the world's clocks from twelve-o'-one
And blow out all the candles on my latest birthday cake
I am flammable, inflammable and a shooting star
You can catch me drinking Jager bombs in the darkness with the
    Angel of Death
And silently smiling on the Bridge of Sighs
Titan! We are all foreigners in most places

This train is bound for glory

One Day or Day One

One day or day one, you decide
You have to feel the energy running through all of your body
If you want to walk on a tightrope to the moon
The way that Freddie Mercury did
One day or day one
You decide!
Greatness only comes before hustle in the dictionary
And everything you can dream of is true
Impossible is just a knave's opinion
One day or day one
The sand is drifting through the hourglass
The winter tide starts to submerge my half-naked body
And I know now that I am ready to make the decision

The Red Sky

The morning sky was red
Like a Status Quo song
By late morning all the larks had ascended
My window of magnificence
Which had served as a mirror in the night-time
Now beckoned me to wake her from her night-shift slumber

She opened her nurse's eyes and brown met blue
For the first tender moments of the day
Neither of us said a word for at least ten minutes
I bind myself to this joy
And a winged life
Beckoned for both of us for eternity

Fifth Season

Spring summer autumn winter
I wish I could get off the treadmill
I am going to create a fifth season
The folk singers are a dying breed in 2021
Cherish the stalwarts growing old
It is all up to you
Stand out on the lonesome highway
Contemplate, speculate and meditate
Over a fifth season coming soon.

Let Johnny Cash be the agitator
Of all your chords and the truth
Let Van Morrison grump his way onto the stage of the
    Manchester Apollo
Singing about no more lockdowns in 2021
And the left-wing protesters march down Cross Street
Representing a blood-stained time and place
As Afghanistan scares us all into crying in our sleep
Writing down those zen dreams at the moment that we wake up
There will be riots coming on the 31st of September
Heralding us into that fifth season.

A soldier of peace walks down Princess Street
Is that a bomb or Black Box's 'Ride on Time' in his backpack?
Out of our heads
Past our peaks
Intertwined in the dark Manchester night
We stumble blindly yet excitedly
Into that dangerous fifth season

Tucson, Arizona

Hey Joey
Your reputation is on the line once and for all
Did you convince yourself of your zenith yet?
Zenith, yeah zenith
Punk rock reached its zenith in London in 1977
But Joey in the desert night at the intersection
Not far from main street
In Tucson, Arizona
Ripped jeans, leather jacket but no visible tattoos
Take the back road
And look up at the stars in the blazing heat desert sky
The stars
That are like renegade diamonds cut out of the evening cumulus clouds
Tall and gawky and creating thunderstorms
As you stare up at that sky
And think of all the tangible successes of your life
Yet the terror of an uncertain ageing future
Don't give the ghost up
You are tall and gawky and creating thunderstorms
And you are going to remain that way
My inspiration in Tucson, Arizona

Vienna Stadtpark

I felt Johann Strauss glaring down at me
"My statue symbolises my achievements,"
He whispers at me
"What did you achieve?"
And I eat my Stracciatella ice cream in a cone
And pace my way over to Stephensplatz
And google 'bands from Vienna'
And nothing I have ever heard of comes up

Past Fledermaus
The street singers and vanilla violinists
Stopping and watching the horse-drawn carriages of tourist shells
And into the Bockshorn Irish Pub
Like a refugee running from my past

It could be 2019 again
At times it feels as if the pandemic never happened
Eighteen months of water treadmills and fracking in my brain
This dream is all about September
September
The most important month always
New beginnings and closed chapters
Surrounded by Jameson and Guinness emblems
I feel comforted
And I reject Johann Strauss's words
I vow to visit the actress lounge after nine o'clock
Take a pie in the face and stay humble

September

September
Pretend that you owe me nothing
The way a smile forgives a mirror
September
The ending and the beginning
This is when life intensifies and crystallises
This is when everything gets real serious
And our Lord is away on business

September
Twenty summers and twenty falls
Angels fall faithlessly into their armchairs
Stay focused
Say no
Make wise choices
In September

There are a lot of confused souls out there
The woke police gather sycophants
Brexit emboldens the racist little minds
People need to feel better than someone
Don't get sucked in
My heart seeks conclusion
In all of this confusion around
Dismiss the gaslighters and the nightwatchman
The moon is dancing purple
And I have to stay a lonesome calculating gambler
The ending and the beginning
God I love you, September

It Doesn't Matter Anymore

The jukebox is playing our favourite song
'It Doesn't Matter Anymore'
I will never forget to remember about you
My dad

The television screen is playing our favourite movie
Butch Cassidy and the Sundance Kid
I will never forget to remember about you
My dad

A replacement I will never be able to find
Drifters hover over my lonely bed
My favourite phrase is 'everything else'
And my favourite person is dead

Russian Roulette

If you can't picture her throwing a Molotov
She ain't the one for you
I need a beautiful malady
And a trans girl to play Russian roulette with tomorrow night

It smells like a bunch of liberals in here
Clap your hands
Clap your hands
Clap your hands and run out of time in Philadelphia
You will all go to heaven
In a rubber dinghy captained by Bill Clinton

What if we kissed in the darkness?
I love everything about you that hurts
Life is tragic because the earth turns
The fire next time
Will be between you and I
But together, Ramona, we can create
A world that is going on underground

Create Something Today

"Create something today,"
She told me
"Even if it sucks."
OK, I thought to myself
Don't worry about the army
Don't worry about the cancer
Don't worry about Boris Johnson
Don't worry about Rupert Murdoch
Don't worry about Jair Bolsonaro
Don't worry about climate change
Don't worry about the next death
Don't worry about the Australian borders staying shut
Don't worry about the next pandemic
Don't worry about the winter months
Don't worry about the debt
Don't worry about the terrorist threat
Give me a pen and paper
Just tie me to an old dead tree
And I will create something today
And I will create something tomorrow
And I will create something every day
Even if it sucks

Goodbye Blue Monday

Goodbye blue Monday
I am too tough to die
Goodbye blue Monday
When giants walked the earth
Goodbye blue Monday
Three chords and the truth
Goodbye blue Monday
I am giving up the toxic for good
Social media cull
No more alcohol
No more energy drinks
Mister Metatone-Berocca-Strepsil-man
No more looking back at mistakes and regrets
Only looking forward now
No more 'Bitter Tears'
No more 'Viva Hate'
The comeback is always more powerful than the setback
The comeback is always more powerful than the setback
The comeback is always more powerful than the setback
Freedom is rejoicing in my hands
And mutates into a wildwood Manchester homecoming
Goodbye blue Monday forever
And please read this at my funeral

Planted Planted Planted

The hanging clouds watch over my bronzed body today
As I try to impress myself each morning in the bathroom mirror
Sometimes when things get really tough
I feel that maybe I have been clumsily buried
But the hanging clouds whisper at me an anonymous
    proposition
Actually, my autumn friend, you have been skilfully planted
Do not complain that you do not have enough time
You have the same number of days in the year as Salvador Dalí
You have the same number of hours in a day as Charles Dickens
You have the same number of minutes in the hour as John
    Lennon
You have the same number of seconds in a minute as Nina
    Simone
In Chinese the word 'crisis' is made up of two characters
One represents danger and one represents opportunity
And you are planted planted planted, my bulletproof friend

My Bulletproof Friend

My bulletproof friend wears a bulletproof vest
In a bulletproof diner in the tougher part of the city
His bulletproof face lets out a bulletproof smile
As his bulletproof legs take him back to his bulletproof
    apartment on the twentieth floor

He plays his bulletproof forty-fives on his bulletproof record
    player
As the werewolves on the street outside howl and beckon into
    the Halloween night
He spoke to no one today
He spoke to no one yesterday

He just ate three bulletproof diner meals a day
Read his bulletproof books of Kerouac, Ginsberg and Burroughs
And played his bulletproof albums of Bowie, Buckley and Brel
And did a bulletproof walk to and fro
And slept a bulletproof uninterrupted sleep each night

My bulletproof friend
Is my imaginary friend
My bulletproof friend
Is who I will become
If only I could be bulletproof

My City Is a Question Mark

My city is a question mark
That I pondered and contemplated
As I spent the day in bed
No television, no kettle, no microwave
You are either blue or red in my city
And you either look back or you look forward

It is funny how the war went on, without Roy and Don
Without Roy and Don
It is funny how the war went on, without Roy and Don
Without Roy and Don

The crowds are back in the nightclubs
And the sporting venues and the electrifying streets
But my city is a question mark
Yes, we know how you will vote at the next election
Oh, suffer little children
And yes, we know how you will celebrate your past glories
With 'Be Here Now' blasting out of the Egerton Arms Hotel
And yes, we know that tabletops are only meant for dancing on
Strangeways prison, here we all come
But we all have to look to the future now
Move on
Shed our old skins
Reinvent ourselves
Explode out into the great big asylum
Shouting our sins out loud
And going out there to sin again

But what if I want to come back?
Back to my home city when so many have left it
And I am left eating rag pudding in the hills
What then, my city?

My city is a question mark

Positive Street

I need something to distract me from the pain
I need something to keep me positive for the future
A simple engraving in Heaton Park will do
So, I took the test
And it came back positive
And I felt positive

The falcon has flown out of the orchard now
And I am sat here surrounded by long grass
With a small primary school pond on one side
There is a tombstone near the entrance
And in the sunshine, I walk over
And start the engraving
This is my territory
Losing myself like Pirsig in the process
As if I had lived on Positive Street my whole life

As I finished my work the falcon returned
And perched on the high, daunting hedge above me
Looking down like a headmaster ritual
Together we approved of the writing
CORPUS CHRISTI
I walked away in silence
And I left the orchard and walked onto the street
Feeling positive

Still Snowing in Bergen

It is still snowing in Bergen
There is a legion of wolves in the forest
They are swelling in number
And growing hungry for blood
As we freewheel, smiling, into the deadly fifth season

George Orwell understood and predicted
Where Western society was heading
But I am happy now
The future and the past can coexist in Norway
As the snow falls down with relentless beauty

Emma, Emma, wherever I may find you
Rebel from the waist down
Give me your thought crimes
Meet me in the snow
And we will run away like bad actors
We won't have children
But our futures are bright together
You will find us in far-off places
And we will only build bridges, not walls
Ole out
Ole out
Ole out
You are going to miss me when I am gone
The tallest man on earth
Acapella quest for technicolour dreamscapes
Walking into the 1980s glistening sea

The ultra-vivid lament
The twenty-first century is roaring into life now
And it is still snowing on us in Bergen

Cobwebs of Your Mind

Firestarter
Firestarter
Staring out at the green Somerset fields
As the gloaming embraces those of us who would testify
Ba ba ba boom
Ba ba ba boom
I need a real firestarter
To take me back through the cobwebs of my mind

Memories of a sun-drenched festival
On the ancient-time land
That was walked on by Lady Guinevere
Get up and get involved
Get up and beat your mental demons
Get up, stand up
Ba ba ba boom
I need a real firestarter
To take me back through the cobwebs of my mind

Brush the cobwebs away
And you will see Jeff Buckley with his 'Mojo Pin'
Jimmy Page and Robert Plant and no quarter
Wallace and Gromit's wrong trousers
And Jarvis Cocker reading us his shopping list
It was one helluva scene

A place to come of age
In 1995
Again and again and again
In 1995
Light the fire
In the top field
The way that Joe Strummer used to
And we can save ourselves together
Take me back through the cobwebs of my mind

Salford Snowfall

Snow falls hard on the Salford ground in late November
More than twelve months have passed now
And we are into the fifth season
The winter of white uncertainty

Ewan McColl painted the hardship
L.S. Lowry wrote down the myriad of character thoughts
You don't remember what to say
You don't remember what to do
At this time of year there is an icy clarity to life
You hold yourself accountable for forward momentum
You can set the tone for the following year
Visible-breath martyrs congregate on Spinningfield surfaces
And the River Irwell gushes and flows too in time to your
    ambitions
Album after album after album in the warm apartment
The caged bird is singing inside your head
On the cusp of December
The Christmas markets whisper your future name
And the name you will give to your newborn

It is all out there really
Everything you would need to look at to write a poem
You don't remember where you have been
And you don't remember who to choose

You wheel
You feel
You steal
You kneel down
And your jeans become wet and cold
In the November Salford snowfall

The Comeback Kid

Loved ones die
People forget all the good early intentions we had
Politicians and the media constantly lie to us
Our health fails us
A friend betrays us through avarice

But the comeback can be more powerful than the setback
The comeback can be more powerful than the setback
If you can convince yourself you are the Comeback Kid
Like Muhammad Ali in Kinchasa, Zaire
Or Joe Montana for the 49ers
Write your own narrative now
And repeat it over and over to yourself and others
Your repeated narrative becomes your powerful truth

The way that we rise under the constant stress
Is the writing brilliantly etched onto our gravestones

Boats to Build

The river doesn't want me today
I turn on my heels back into the inviting gloom
Krishna River with your source by the Mahabaleshwar

The river didn't want me last month
When I cried out lonesome at the sky
Missouri River with your source at Brower's Spring

The river didn't want me last year either
As I confessed all my sins to a chosen sister
Murray River with your source in the Australian Alps

We have boats to build, brother
New adventures to waltz into
We have boats to build, brother
With new heroes as yet unannounced
We have boats to build, brother
As Uncle Walt guides us through the leaves of grass

Ocean Beach

I am going to go back to Cow Records
With a tender SoCal excitement gang
And one day make immortal purchases
And sing to the ocean
And hear the ocean roar
Afterwards I will walk up to you
On Newport Avenue and ask,
"Is it all over? Can we go home now?"
As the pilgrims in Coca-Cola black shuffle away
And illuminated by the glow of a full moon, you will answer
That the battle rages on
That proud hearts beat more than ever
That the Electric Waste Band is by no means done yet
But you are here to tell me that it is Easter Day

Collette

The First Lady of Manchester
Kisses like her life depends on it
Met her in 42nd Street with her sister
Taught me that Derby Day wasn't a horse race
She rocks like Phil Lynott
And she rolls like Keith Richards
Ain't no one good enough for her in my eyes
Especially not yours truly

Collette, Collette, Collette
The best a man can get
Kisses like her life depends on it
Can structurally analyse me inside and out
Accepts me for my waywardness and drunkenness
And still comes as my date to a Slade Xmas gig at The Ritz

The First Lady of Manchester
Is too good and pure for this world
She could lasso the moon and surrounding stars
And inspire her Irish cousins to vacate the dive bars
She will get to heaven alright
A dazzling, spectacular but bruised soul
If she could coach me and cajole me and take me with her
Don't want to go there on my own (it would be boring)
But if I could go there with her, that would be my life goal

The Quiet One

The boys at work in Nottingham city centre call her The Quiet One
And she passes under the radar most weeks
But she gives me hope and energy
Because I see in her the bright future of a less confused world

Folks can judge and pontificate and spew
On Twitter or Facebook or wherever they see fit
But they who have not sinned should cast the first stone
They who have never lived properly can try to condemn the
    whole world to death
Her kindness is not a weakness

She might not be a chatterbox queen
But she can talk with her eyes and her smile
She gives me hope of a better world in the 2030s
She isn't quiet; everyone else is too loud

At the photocopier or the coffee machine
She brightens up my drab days
Her existence comforts like Dave Brubeck's 'Take Five'
I don't want to work from home thanks, Boris
I need to see her and hear her and feel her consistent daily
    presence
Maybe even meet her by the lions on Market Square
Before a quiet drink in The Bell Inn or The Royal Children
Now I am getting older and quieter too (thank the heavens) and
    kinder
And one day I hope that she will notice that in me too

That Subverted Bayeux Tapestry

That subverted Bayeux Tapestry
Descends into urban concept album masterpieces
Harald taking an arrow in the eye
At the end of the rainbow
He could be happy ever after

Them advanced Rachmaninov concertos
Ascend into spinning mirage desert daffodil plantations in the sky
Caught in a tornado I may die
Somewhere over the rainbow
He could be happy ever after

Them Birmingham Six head over heels
Vibrate into vigilante attacks on suspected nymphomaniacs
Until her heart actually breaks in slow motion
Displaying all of the colours of the rainbow
She could be happy ever after

Them Shocking Blue Dutch 'Love Buzz' brokers
Waltz down Wall Street seducing the Princess of Crown Heights
Try conning Saint Peter three times
Rainbow Nation – the greater your storm the brighter your rainbow
She could be happy ever after

Them aeolian cadences sung by eunuchs
Make martyrs out of the canvassing team on Mollergata
We all trade blood oaths of commitment
The crock of gold is at the end of the rainbow
We could be happy ever after

Boys and Girls in Manchester

Boys and girls in Manchester can shape the new world
They can take their sadness and pain
And collectively use it to break free from their pasts
They can hold the new dawn accountable
Entwined Canal Street lovers
For a world where only poetry, defiance and truth will reign
They can be universal in sympathy
And help lift up the marginalised and discriminated against
    daily

They must not give way to sophistication
And submit to the money-go-round and conformity
They must have real straight talk about souls
For every day is precious and every stranger's smile is sacred
Aspiring artists and musicians in Hulme, Rusholme and Salford
Hold on and channel your sadness and pain
You are the greatest hope of civilisation
Boys and girls in Manchester can shape the new world

Mr Clean

I don't care much for the man who has worn a suit to work every
    day on Bishopsgate
I lose interest quickly in the salesman with the tie
The 'married at 25' people-pleaser who walks without thinking
Past the homeless man who served in the war

I like the desperate madmen growling at the moon at night
    outside Camden Town station
Too much heart, too much feeling, too much experimentation
Explosive lives led
Raw passions indulged
Loves lost and battles fought
First there is an opportunity, then there is a betrayal
First there is an opportunity, then there is a betrayal
Leave me alone with these men
Tomorrow night the streets are ours

Refuse to Bend

Stay away from people who always feel they have to be in the crowd
Stay away from people always obsessed with the latest market trend
'Super Black Market Clash'
'1-2 Crush on You'
Stay away from people who spend too much of their time on Twitter
Stay away from people who have an OnlyFans account
'Super Black Market Clash'
'1-2 Crush on You'

Just search deep inside yourself
And find the thing you truly love
And follow it
Follow it all the way until the end
Until you want the part of it that it refuses to give
And refuse to bend
And refuse to stop
And follow it all the way until it kills you

Living in New York City

Living in New York City
Living in New York City
The crisp January walks into Fort Greene Park
There is a lot of love and hate here
Life can be a mirror
If you frown at it, it frowns back;
If you smile, it returns the compliment

An East Village bar crawl is best completed alone
Start off at the Double Down Saloon and end up doing the
 triangle of doom
But keep an infinite mindset
Or you end up like Joey Ramone
He never really got out of New York
He never really got out of the East Village
Or you end up like Ryan Adams wishing he was one of The
 Strokes
And coming across like a hexagon of doom
That you don't want to meet in the bathroom

Living in New York City
Living in New York City
Yvette writes indestructible poetry over in Queens
Leonora is the everlasting meditating goddess from
    Turkmenistan
Loving people one tasty dish at a time
The tantra connection she has to Lou Reed
Will manifest itself in a Coney Island eatery in 2023

The humid Manhattan June evening is something I have
    conquered the third time around
The compassion in this city
Can be peeled back and revealed layer by layer
Year by year
As long as you keep a writer's mind on the subway
Post lyrics in the Iroquois Hotel lobby
And pay regular visits to the Bell House in Gowanus
Or Brooklyn Steel, as John the Baptist
Preparing everyone for the next British Invasion

Cobwebs and Strange Spiders

So sad about us
We didn't have to break up
A cobweb is a spider web
And ours was a strange one too
'Cobwebs' is a song by The Coral from 'Roots and Echoes'
And theirs was a strange one too
Cobweb is a character in *Midsummer Night's Dream*
And they were a strange one too

So sad about us
We didn't have to break up
Somehow, we lost our way
In transatlantic fury
We each welcomed a knave into the slipstream
We each lost our perspective on the sober endgame
There is a chance we could get it back
One of us has to cross that ocean
Comeback Kid
I am dreaming of you and me
I am dreaming of a new cobweb and a strange spider

My Wartime Jacket

There will soon be a time
When there will be nobody alive left
Who remembers the war
Storming the beaches
And listening to Vera Lynn

There will soon be a day
When the last allied soldier has died
And all that remains are their black-and-white photos
And the blood-red poppy fields
And the etchings on the silver graves of no love lost

When that day comes
I will put on my wartime jacket
Grease back my wavy head of hair
Reconnect with my 1952 Vincent Black Lightning
And ride the coastal road from Brighton to Hastings

That day will be momentous
That day will be joyous
That day will come soon

Lord Byron

Lord Byron, you were the first true rock star
Nurtured so close to Southwell Minster
So close to my Nottingham student days
I can see it in your aspect and your eyes
Court the London fame
Then turn your back and go into voluntary exile
Join the Greek war of independence with fatal results
Glenarvon
Lord Ruthven
Mr Rochester
Heathcliff even
Byronic heroes all
Convinced that the floor is lava
With idealised and flawed character
Great talent
Great passions
Distaste for conventions
No respect for privilege and rank
Thwarted in love
Banging your head against a tree in exile
Until it bleeds love and procreation
A secret past mixed with overconfidence
A self-destructive manner
Like Elvis, Jim Morrison and Phil Lynott
But in Venice, Ravenna and Pisa
George Gordon Byron
Your thirty-six years you lived well

A Fierce Friend

You are a fierce friend
You are the rainbow in my sky
You have fifteen talents
All invisible to the naked eye

Inca girl in the skinny kitchen
You make me a better poet
You dance truth in sunshine riots
And your written name meanders through the lonesome clouds

Still you are a fierce friend to me
As love is confusing to my soul
You provide shelter to the rebels
A higher ground and a duet as the ultimate goal

Never Gonna Retire

Jimmy is never gonna retire
Just like Clint Eastwood
He will always have boats to build
Memories of graveyards
Memories of old tombs
Waves of longing
Each day is the first day in a new job
And his spirit is the surge of the raging ocean

Switched off sometimes
Insomnia sometimes
He is the same person he was in the summer of 2005
They say that hope is happiness
And happiness is more important than pleasure
I find comfort in old Jimmy
Who is never gonna retire

This One Is Optimistic

There are deep rivers ahead
For the ideal girl
In London from Manchester
New haircut, new tattoo, new beginning
Hallelujah
She reaches thirty
Practises yoga now
And stretches her arms (with eyes closed) to the curving sky

Born in Guinea-Bissau
Psychology graduate
Well travelled but hurting
Founded and leads a non-profit organisation
Her future life is direct action
Good news awaits
Songs of freedom await
"Who will police the police?" she asks
Although she won't bring the missing back
She will shake many things up for the better
For her sisters in the storm
For the living dead
This one is optimistic

Sex Beats the Devil

"What are your favourite numbers?"
The ice queen tabloid music journalist asked me
Whilst plucking dismissively at the ten segments of her dying tangerine

"That is easy
Sixty-six and sixty-nine,"
I replied with no eye contact

Sixty-six:
'Revolver'
'Aftermath'
'Blonde on Blonde'
'Pet Sounds'
'Freak Out!'
'The Sound of Silence'
'The Psychedelic Sounds of the 13th-Floor Elevators'
'A Quick One'

Sixty-nine:
'Tommy'
'Let It Bleed'
'Abbey Road'
'Five Leaves Left'
'Led Zeppelin Two'
'Liege & Lief'
'Bayou Country'
'At San Quentin'
'The Velvet Underground'
'Everybody Knows This Is Nowhere'

I look her in the eye now and smile
"It's a close contest to be fair
But sex beats the devil every time."

2022

In 2022 I will shoot to kill
I will be away a while
But I will come back to see you in:
January
February
March
April
May
JUNE
July
And we can climb the Glastonbury Tor a few days after summer solstice
The lyrics to Joy Division songs have described my life for the last five and a half years
But as the mist rolls off the violent sea
And surrounds the bleak house we are both snuggled into
I need you to look deeply into my eyes
It is the only way you will know
If I am telling the truth

Downstream

My muse floats downstream watching me
Half-submerged in the River Irwell
A pulse
I know I am not dreaming
A bomb
Lies ahead
A waterfall of opportunity
I watch her continue to float
On this January day
Her beautiful face
Her dark hair with strands of grey
It is just the two of us
And I start walking alongside her
Crossing bridges
Passing The Lowry Hotel
Passing Leftbank Apartments
But she gets lost in the reeds
Nothing to see here
I fear the ice age is coming
For she can be my muse no more
I return to my Salford home
And start painting a shipwreck
A self-portrait
To give me hope when the world reaches a new normal
The phone rings
It is the Devil
I decide to confront him and make conversation

You Can Hear the Bombers Overhead

We need to make poetry out of our daily agony
If not, we will start hearing the bombers overhead
We will start visualising them digging the cemetery graves
With Joe Strummer standing in the grave
When I say we
I am celebrating the existence of you and I
The sky is crying
For former pageant material
And a bandaged hobo who stole a Cadillac
And drove it from Austin
Through Waco
To Dallas
And lost all his money at Lone Star Park
The poetry will be derivative of Walt Whitman
And we will fit together like a jigsaw puzzle

Bacchanalia

I listen to 'The Queen Is Dead' by The Smiths
Most Monday afternoons when the sky is grey
And I remember that I have had
Too many drinks
Too many women
Too many books
Too many songs
Too many films
Too many car journeys
Too many flights
Too many rock concerts
Too many winning bets

I feel more like Cleopatra than Enobarbus
Ambulances of hate passed me by
From Piccadilly Gardens to the Sunset Strip

In the future I will live by the coast
And dream up magnificent sea battles
And listen to 'Southpaw Grammar' for the first time

Whiskey Man

He aimed to drink all the brands of whiskey
From Jameson to Johnnie Walker
From Southern Comfort to Chivas Regal
Until he discovered himself comatose
And in bed with the biggest floozy of them all:
Himself

But he didn't die in the end
When he recognised his own reflection
Instead, he sobered up
Wrote a letter each to his brother and mother
Bought a new guitar from Blues City Music
And boarded the ten-thirty Greyhound to Nashville

Alana, the Gangster's Beautiful Daughter

Alana, the imprisoned gangster's beautiful daughter,
Saw beauty in everyday things
And told me there were good things out there if you looked for them
She had fake tan and a curvy figure
Stood five feet ten
Long blonde hair and long nails
Eyebrows plucked
And leopard-skin bandana on
Smoked cigarettes
Drank rum and coke
Was attracted to tall, skinny men, but stayed single
Was a committed humanist who had survived a car crash on the M42
Alana lingered for buskers on Lister Gate
Cried in the Savoy cinema
Fed the birds in Forest Fields
And raised money for a homeless charity every week
She had Toulouse-Lautrec posters on her bedroom wall
Prayed daily for her father's early release
But the albatross hung motionless in the West Bridgford sky above her

She is ageing now
Still a fierce and resplendent sight on my pavement
As she walks home after midnight
And my dwarf-like body yearns for her heart

Sometimes when I get too overcome with longing
I spend the whole day in my bedroom listening to Tom Waits
    albums on repeat, thinking about her

Set the House Ablaze

I was surrounded by fear and prejudice
White skinheads dancing to 'Train to Skaville'
Where does the hate stem from?
I see someone looking different and I want to be them
You are frightened by skin darker than yours
Frightened of what?
That your monotone life might be exposed
That you haven't got the talent that you wanted
Most people hunt in packs
And find something to mock
In packs
Why not be an outsider
And universal in sympathy?
Veiled threats
And karma regrets
I am going to speak out
Your hate won't win through tonight

The first half of life is learning to be an adult
Learning the racism
The second half of life we should try to be a child again
Uniting through tenderness and Pete Seeger songs

A Collector

Sunshine girl brings rainclouds
You are a different kind
Because you wanted my mind
Once manipulated fully
You could make a cosy nest in there
Haunting my stairways
Stepping outside sometimes
And sleeping in my hat

Spot the weirdos
You gloated when we went on holiday
And showered me with fake friendship
You were a different kind
Because you wanted my mind
We wrestled over it
But I wouldn't give it fully
Then all of a sudden you turn on me
Over practically nothing
A trifle
'La Donna e Mobile'
And you never speak to me again
I guess I learned you were a collector
You were a different kind
Because you wanted my mind
You are the Queen of Darkness
You are the Butterfly Collector!

37 Miracles

What can an artist do without pain and heartache?
He or she needs it just as much as a laptop these days
Did someone break your heart?
Just a little
Maybe you needed it
Just a little
Go home
And memorise the 37 miracles
And then we can talk again at Ditto Coffee on Oxford Street
    tomorrow

Consistency

With consistency (and calculated daring)
You can end up bearing witness
To the funeral pyre of your nemesis

Time Is Tight

There will be a day
Not too far into the future
(And it is approaching faster than you realise)
When the material winners
Will be left with a bankrupt soul
And those dedicated to uplifting others
The nurses
The teachers
The social workers
The support workers
The charity workers
The counsellors
Will be declared the winners
And embrace each other
And feel the warm glow of the sun
Time is tight
But it is never too late to jump on the train

San Francisco Nights

I wander up Haight-Ashbury late into the evening
After a daytime spent hustling in the Castro and Tenderloin
Eventually sitting on my own in the darkness in Golden Gate Park
War! You talk to me of it
The only war that matters is the one against creativity
An army! My friend has gone to join it
An army is an army against love

Lawrence Ferlinghetti opened the City Lights Bookstore in 1953
The first bookshop in the United States
Devoted entirely to paperbacks
And the San Francisco Renaissance had begun
Sitting alone in the darkness is like sitting inside the Trojan Horse
I am ready now for my own battle
To keep the renaissance going in 2022
This is how Ginsberg ended up
Alone and howling at his messed-up life
More like 'Cortez the Killer' than Buddha
I need volunteers to help me now
Who will come forward?
I will teach them of the bodhisattvas
And the Four Noble Truths
(And maybe some more)
Come sit with me in the darkness in Golden Gate Park tonight

Sourdough Mountain

I climbed up Sourdough Mountain and watched the sunrise
Believing I saw the reincarnation of Robert Frost
On the Desolation Peak
I wanted to set myself on fire with a can of kerosene
Like the Buddhist monk on the front cover of the Rage Against
    the Machine album
But I remembered that in reading more books I could find inner
    peace
In writing more poetry I could settle with my demons

The sky above me is just the reflection of a newly formed puddle
The forests are our undreamt nightmares with fertiliser on top
The ocean is a collection of lovers we forgot to seduce
The sun is a tangerine peel playing charades on Christmas Day

I wrote and wrote until lunchtime
Alone with my thoughts on Sourdough Mountain
And it felt really pure and good
This evening I will go back to my temporary abode
And watch a film about Andy Warhol and Edie Sedgwick
Valhalla, I am coming…

New York City Poem Number Five

Most people only come here for a week or two of their lives
Walk in Central Park
See the Statue of Liberty
Take pictures at the top of the Empire State Building
I lived here alone
And I understand now why the Bible is the way it is
A city photographed by a Nazi
Raindrops and looking beyond the guidebooks
I liked the Stonewall Inn on a Saturday night
The Dead Poet Pub
Physical Graffitea
53rd and 3rd
Strawberry Fields in the gloaming
The small-town heroes and heroines of Murray Hill
A beautiful lady near Ditmars Boulevard, Astoria
Who read Charles Dickens at eleven years old
I tried to go deeper than the film scenes
But I only scratched the surface
But I dig and I dig and I dig
And sitting in Redemption on Third Avenue
The next New York City awaits me

Dear Young Writers Quarterly

Dear Young Writers Quarterly,
I am hoping you might publish some of my short stories
I am not that young anymore
But I am targeting your magazine now instead of flying to Moscow
Because I heard some of the publishers over there are paedophiles
I am not a paedophile
But Lewis Carroll probably was
And things turned out alright for him (which makes me sad)
Albert Camus was a total arsehole
Yet the critics went crazy for his writing
I am not a total arsehole
But I do have a pet parrot
That says 'Some Girls Are Bigger Than Others'
Every time a female walks into the room
I have an Instagram account @dicktheshit2
And I am enclosing all my short stories about the city of Dublin
James Joyce, go eat your heart out, motherfucker
Yours sincerely,
Phil Lynott's youngest half brother
P.S. I once starred in a gay sado-masochistic porn film, but it can't be found on Pornhub
So should have little bearing on my aspiring literary career

Tomorrow Is a Long Time Away

Let's make love now, Angelina
Tomorrow is a long time away
I may have a cardiac arrest before then
And you may have to leave and return to your hometown
It has been hard times living in this grey city
Through the lockdowns and the lies and the false starts
Let's make love now
Tomorrow is a long time away
Today feels like spaghetti junction
Unless we go into the bedroom and lock the door
Breathe into each other's mouths
Listen to each other's heartbeats
Start ascending the paths to the summit

There will be no more rejoicing after we are parted
This moment could be as beautiful and unheralded as a fleeting
    rainbow
Volcanoes and earthquakes, we could start them all
Then hide away denying all knowledge
Finally, when we are lying entangled in each other's sweat
We can discuss at length the last thoughts of Edgar Allan Poe
And I will still love you tomorrow morning and the mornings
    after

This House Is Rocking

This house is rocking
So don't bother knocking
Inside they play sea shanties and pirate ballads
Of the dead bootleggers of Boston
I waited by a bulletproof window
I am the last of the hellraisers
I drink to Homer's lament
I drink to Apollo; I drink to Zeus
I hold Ian Curtis lyrics in my hand
Travelling with a sweet hitch-hiker
Hunting Dean Moriarty in Salford
I dreamt of Sydney Carton
Whilst leaning against the John Ryland library
And weeping
The Chinese New Year and icicles light up St. Ann's Square
I hear a spontaneous requiem for the Cherokee girl
Who chases the ghosts of America into the darkness
For ever and ever
Hurtling towards the coyote boundary of city and country
Past the Mohawks
Past the Senecas
Past the Iroquois
Ready now for the funeral stomp

Salford, North-West England, February 2022

Meeting Fast Eddie tonight and seeing a Clash tribute band at Rebellion
He took a power nap and when he woke up it was 1977 all over again
I created a drop-out zone in my apartment off Chapel Street
Surrounded myself with Spike Lee films and Allen Ginsberg poetry
Surrounded myself with Steve Earle albums and Simon Sinek quotes
Dreamed about beatniks, fanatics, loners and angel heads
The whiskey is out of my system fully
Less YouTube, less easy access, less late-night dread
More flash fiction writing, more punk and folk music, more physical meditation and yoga
Bold plans and bright futures with lists

Sat with Charlotte and she told me there are more revolutions coming
As Angela Rayner leads the enlightenment
And the noticeboard of the King's Arms, Salford
Accompanied by the jukebox sounds of John Cooper Clarke and Nico
Stretched out on heroin and brave jolts of speed
Tells of all our future renaissances
"You can do it all yourself," I tell myself
Write another poem, walk back to my Salford apartment
And remind myself not to confuse sex with love
Or love with happiness
As the evening raindrops flush away the worst memories of dark nights of the soul

Lone Star State Girl

As darkness sleeps over another Manhattan ice blast
And the icicles have got into my ears and my new gloves
I walk past Bryant Park
Where I never enjoyed any peace of mind
The Rockefeller Centre smiled at me once
Trump Towers
A homage to a toxic crock of shit
And Fifth Avenue bustles me away
Until the gloom starts to bite at my brain
Every February is a brutal month
You have to deal with these winter winds
And the dark slush and the ice and the snow

Time to move to Austin, Texas
Sit at the bar of the Texas Chili Parlor
Come on in, y'all
There is a Lone Star State friend waiting for me there

Plodding Wins the Race

Stay focused on a straight line
Like a Viking longship from Reykjavik
Plodding wins the race

Ignore the gaslighters
Visualise the Albion island of your future
Plodding wins the race

Beware not to take a nap
Or become tempted by the siren call
Plodding wins the race

A divine power looks over you
Musicians know, short story writers know, Aesop knows
Plodding wins the race

Like a Butterfly at Night

'Find what you love and let it kill you' – Charles Bukowski.

My name is Eva Braun and tomorrow I am going to marry Adolf Hitler, the man I have loved all these years. I have loved him since I first met him as a teenager.

There are April showers outside, but they will clear tomorrow and in truth they are making me the happiest woman alive. The rain cleanses any imperfections from my soul and readies me for the big event. Here in the Führerbunker there are no windows, but I decide to climb the stairs and step outside into the wet day. The puddles of water on the concrete road glitter with shades of grey, yellow and green.

I walk further than I should, and I know I am at risk, but tomorrow is the 29th of April 1945 and I feel destiny calling out to me and daring me to be braver than ever before. I have no camera on me, and I can take no photographs today. The cyanide capsules in the right pocket of my brown coat feel smooth across my painted fingertips and the feel of them jolts electricity up my arm and through my entire splendid Aryan body. Reading this you must have hope. The day after the 29th of April is the 30th of April. The day after the 30th of April is the 1st of May. It is the same every year. They say that the Red Army troops are near. You must have hope.

I was born in Munich and my mother was a schoolteacher. I have two sisters, Ilse and Gretl, the first one older and the second younger. When I was seventeen, I started working as a photographer for Heinrich Hoffmann, the official photographer for the Nazi Party. Adolf was twenty-three years older than me, but the moment I met him I fell in love. He had been living with his half-niece at the time and she had just committed suicide, leaving him vulnerable and emotionally confused, in a way that others couldn't see, but I instantly connected with. He was drawn to strength, and he was drawn to the drama of near-death experiences. I faked a suicide attempt at an early stage to draw him closer and it worked. By 1932 I had his full devotion, the devotion of a man who was destined to become the most powerful in the world. That devotion was better than all the photographs in the world. That devotion made my life wonderful.

As I keep walking now, further and further away from the Reich Chancellery Garden, I grab a tight hold of the letter that is in my left hand. I know I am closer and closer to the letter box now and I lengthen my strides with purpose. The letter must not get too wet though and so I push it back into my coat pocket.

A guard sees me now and walks over with an umbrella.

"Do you need any help, madam?"

"I am fine, thank you, in spite of the rain."

"If you stand still for one minute, I will fetch you an umbrella, to make your walk more pleasant."

He suspects nothing and performs his chivalrous act in sixty seconds.

As I walk now with the umbrella, the rain seems to stop, and I am overcome by a feeling that the season has changed. Summer had given way to autumn, then winter had kept us all on our guard. When winter ended spring teased us with false hope and orgasm denial, but now the season was changing again, and I didn't know what to expect from a fifth season. All I could think was that I had to post the letter. Nothing would be safe in the future until the letter was inside the letter box.

I often stayed overnight at his Munich apartment when he was in town and then I would travel with him as the official photographer of the Nazi Party.

My second suicide attempt was in 1935. He simply wasn't giving me enough attention and months had gone by since we had last made love. The near-death drama caused things to improve though and he bought me a new residence in Munich as well as my own special apartment at the Reich Chancellery, designed by Albert Speer. I was untouchable from then on. I attended the Nuremberg rallies, and I developed close relationships with all the important people Adolf had around him. Oh, what a time it was! Berlin hosted the Olympic games, and the late thirties became better and better like a relentless spinning wheel of fortune. I had reached a zenith of happiness by this time.

Of course, Adolf did not want to marry as he felt this might diminish his appeal to the masses in some way. I understood and so I kept a low profile to keep him happy. I wasn't very interested in politics to tell you the truth, and I had no idea what was really going on in the important meetings that occurred, from which I was forbidden to attend. The thing that annoyed me the most was the ban on cosmetics that he was attempting to bring in two years ago, as part of some new economic policy. What a ridiculous idea. I protested, and I got my way; the ban never happened – there was just a temporary halt in cosmetics production instead.

A few tiny raindrops from my umbrella rim are falling on my glasses now as I approach the letter box. Perhaps I should have bought Negus and Stasi with me, but I decided to leave them behind with Blondi, so as not to attract too much attention to myself.

My eyes are now filled with hot tears. All the clocks around the world have stopped and I stand balancing this terrible letter on the edge of the entrance to the letter box. I put my umbrella down and bigger raindrops now splash onto my face and my life.

It is at this moment that I see Adolf out of the corner of my eye walking in my direction. His sturdy physique arouses me, and I think instantly of the passionate sex we had on the sofa in the Munich apartment. The same sofa that Neville Chamberlain was photographed sitting innocently on in all the best English-speaking newspapers.

He stood next to me now and told me we should walk back to the Führerbunker together.

"Joseph Goebbels is arriving in the morning. He will be one of the witnesses at our wedding."

How exciting, I thought to myself. And at thirty-three years old the timing felt absolutely perfect.

We walked back together in love and the sun even came out to herald the fifth season. I never did post the letter to my sister Gretl, and I burnt it that evening in the Führerbunker. No one has ever read its contents.

I prepared everything for Joseph and his family's imminent arrival. There was no more rain that evening or the next day. The day after the 29th of April is the 30th of April. The day after the 30th of April is the 1st of May.

New Year's Eve

'The only true currency in this bankrupt world is what
we share with someone else when we are uncool' –
Philip Seymour Hoffman, *Almost Famous*.

So here we are again on the 31st of December. A life measured out with a finite mindset of three-hundred-and-sixty-five-day chunks. Each year is subject to reviews and post-match analysis in my head. Who was the man of the year, who was the woman of the year and who was the villain of the year? Some years hold magical memories in my head. 1995 – my first Glastonbury Festival, the height of Britpop, leaving home and going to university, coming of age. 2005 – a promotion at work, a beautiful girlfriend, a heatwave summer and blissful road trip adventures.

Now I feel, though, that it is time to embrace the infinite mindset. So, I drive my car to the Severn Bridge and park it at the spot where Richey Edwards would have done all those years ago. Each year blurs into one now and my drive and my focus have gone. Physically, I have let myself go this year. My parents are long gone and the last time I had a girlfriend, a Labour government was still in Downing Street. Working from home every day and too old to go to most of the bars and clubs in the city that I used to love.

In the Gregorian calendar this is the last day of the year. In my head, this could be the last day of my life. Saint Sylvester's Day, they call it in many countries…

As I walk away from my car and lean against the railing at the edge of the bridge, I can see clearly now the gushing grey water below. It has been raining hard for every day of the Merryneum and the river is very high for this time of year. Flood warnings have been repeated on the radio throughout the day for both England and Wales. This is good; this is what I need. I want to jump in, and I want things to end as quickly as possible. What do I have to live for next year? I am never going to have children; I am not going to make any new friends and the ongoing virus is reducing mankind to a watered-down version of its past glories – less human interactions, more submission to right-wing governments, more toxic commentary on social media and a time of less creativity and subversive behaviour. Racism is on the rise everywhere too, fuelled by egotistical leaders like Trump and Bolsonaro. If Adolf Hitler flew in today, they would send a limousine anyway. I read Amanda Gorman's *Call Us What We Carry* the day before yesterday, and I feel now is as good a time as any to bow out. Now is as good a time as any to jump.

In Scotland they call it *Hogmanay*.
In Wales they call it *Calennig*.
In Uzbekistan they call it *Yangi Yil*.
Some African Americans call it *Karamu*.
In Algeria they call it *Reveillon*.
In Russia they call it *Kanun Novogo Goda*.
In Japan they call it *Omisoka*.
The Line Islands of Kiribati and Tonga experience it first.
Baker Island and American Samoa experience it last.

The final day of the Gregorian year. Reflection and revision. Late-night partying and family gatherings. Feasting and fireworks. Countdown and multiple alcoholic beverages. The Severn Bridge and my swansong.

It must be around 11:30pm now, and I walk back to my car and sit inside, and I contemplate Richey Edwards for a while, whilst drinking a can of beer. Each of the first three albums was better than the one before, but 'The Holy Bible' was an absolute masterpiece and all the song lyrics were written by Richey, at a time when he was having severe mental health issues. I put the album on my car's CD player as a reminder. I sit and wonder if he did really kill himself or if he just created the perfect disappearing act and is living somewhere in happiness now.

'Gold Against the Soul' had sounded quite American and a bit too rockist for some. 'The Holy Bible' took the listener back to something a bit more British-sounding.

Listening once again to the album in my freezing white Hyundai car with no one else around, I fully appreciated how this album had been put together with academic discipline.

My mind became filled once again with prostitution, American consumerism, British imperialism, the Holocaust, freedom of speech, self-starvation, the death penalty, serial killers, political revolution, fascism, childhood and suicide.

Maybe this was as far as Richey Edwards' character could go on this planet. There never could have been a sequel to this.

'Yes' contains dialogue from the documentary *Hookers, Hustlers, Pimps and their Johns*.

'Ifwhiteamericatoldthetruthforonedayit'sworldwouldfallapart'.

'Of Walking Abortion' begins with an extract of an interview with Hubert Selby Junior.

'She Is Suffering'. We have to empty ourselves of all desire to achieve truth. It's a Buddhist thing.

'Archives of Pain' deals with the glorification of serial killers and begins with the words of the mother of one of Peter Sutcliffe's victims from a TV report on his trial.

I am five songs in and on my fourth can of lager of the night. It can't yet be midnight and listening to the music is acting as a procrastination tactic for the real reason I am supposed to be here. This is the exact moment that the stranger enters the car and sits down in the passenger seat. The song 'Revol' is just starting; I turn the volume down and, pushing my body against the driver's seat door, I turn to face the long-haired stranger. I can't initially tell if this young person is a man or woman.

"What are you doing sitting in my car?"

"Don't stress; I am a peaceful person. I just sat in here to talk and to get some warmth. I had been listening to the music you were playing for a while, whilst I was standing outside. I understand why you are here."

The stranger had a soft Welsh accent and reminded me of a character out of the film *Submarine* that I had seen a few years before.

"Would you like a beer? It might help to keep you warm. Are you homeless?"

They explained that they had been sleeping rough for most of the year since arguments with their family in South Wales.

The stranger didn't smell of anything and it seemed that the only scent in the car was of the freshly opened Budweiser beer cans.

"Well, Happy New Year," they said to me as they opened the beer can.

"Has it been a good year for you?"

I explained that it hadn't and that I was thinking of killing myself as my life seemed to be getting progressively worse year on year. I talked and talked for around twenty minutes with only the odd prompt or subtle interjection from the stranger. I covered the death of my parents, the break-up with my wife, the alienation I was feeling from old friends and my general discontent with the modern world. The stranger listened and listened and waited until I had burnt myself out.

I took a long swig from my beer can and turned towards the stranger. They were reaching for something in their coat pocket. I felt a slight nervousness that it might be a knife or even a gun, but with great purpose they placed a paperback book onto the dashboard of my car.

"This is *A Tale of Two Cities* by Charles Dickens. I read it for the first time in GCSE English at my school. I have read it many times since. I am going to give you this copy and when I leave the car, I want you to drive back to where you live and read it from cover to cover over the next week. Will you do that for me?"

"But at around midnight I was going to jump off the bridge and kill myself."

"I know you were," whispered the stranger, "but New Year's Eve is over now and from what you have told me, you actually do have a lot to live for. You have a good job, which is more than I do. You have good old friends, you just need to open up to them properly about how you have been feeling recently; you need to reconnect with some of the best of them, who will show they care when they understand how down you have been. You have a warm and safe home to go back to. Again, that is far more than I have. I should be the one jumping off the bridge tonight, but I am not going to."

We sat in silence together for a few more minutes.

"Will you drive home now and go and read the book for me? Please pay close attention to the Sydney Carton character. See how the author portrays him as a scoundrel and a low life initially, but see how his behaviour turns out to be the best of all in the end. Please read it for me."

I shrug my shoulders and reluctantly agree to the stranger's wishes.

"Where will you go tonight?" I enquire.

"Don't worry about me. I have a warm place to go, and I have a mountain of books to get through this year. I have plenty of fictional characters to keep me entertained. And when I have the strength, I come to this spot here and persuade people like you not to kill yourself."

The stranger smiled at me, shook my hand and left the car. They started walking away, but after a few paces turned back and reopened the passenger door slightly.

"Richey didn't kill himself either, you know. He just had to escape all the poison that he saw engulfing him. I will say hello to him from you."

With that, they closed the door and walked away into the cold and wet night.

I felt stunned and didn't move for a while. When I did regain some purpose, I opened the first page of *A Tale of Two Cities*:

It was the best of times, it was the worst of times, it was the age of wisdom, it was the age of foolishness...

I decided to drive home and play a more uplifting album for the journey and selected 'Rust Never Sleeps' by Neil Young. I would start reading the book that the stranger had given to me the next day, and I decided to try to be more grateful for some of the positive things I had in my life, not least my good health, my relatively young age and a set of old friends I had neglected of late.

New Year's Day is the first day of the year in the modern Gregorian calendar. On driving home, I saw some people in fields with rays of light celebrating a northern winter solstice.

In pre-Christian times the day was dedicated to Janus, God of gateways and beginnings.

The early Roman calendar even designated the 1st of March as the first day of the year. *Septem* means seven, right? *Octo* means eight, *novem* means nine and *decem* means ten.

In England they say we only started recognising the 1st of January as the start of a new year in 1752.

In the Gwaun Valley in Wales, the new year is celebrated on the 13th of January. I wonder if my strange friend knew that.

In North and South Korea, New Year's Day is celebrated as *Seollal*.

The Sikh New Year is celebrated on the 14th of March every year, to recognise the birth of Guru Nanak.

In Iran, New Year is celebrated as *Nowruz* and occurs on or around the 21st of March.

I am glad I didn't jump.

Instead, I am able to repeat to you the highest avowal that I can possibly make – *I am still alive*.

I got out of my car in the Jewellery Quarter around 2:30am. With *A Tale of Two Cities* under my arm, I walked into my warm apartment and felt overwhelmed by the immensity of existing things and new things to learn. For the first time in a while, I felt like a sponge trying to saturate itself, smiling because I had noticed for the first time the reflections in my windows and mirrors.

Wild Billy's Circus Story

Circus Town
Billy is travelling across Kansas from one small town to the next. As a machinist on a Ferris wheel with his lover as a fire-eater and his best friend Tommy as a sword-swallower. They tour through the summer heat, getting rapturous applauses from each stop, night after night in the eighties and nineties. Dodging death and living on the edge. Not compensated greatly in dollars but living as lovers under the stars. In the daytime Marie and Billy practise their routines and then retire to their bunks and listen to Mötley Crüe, Poison, Quiet Riot and Skid Row. They debate for hours which band is the best, even in the midst of making love and creating pools of sweat that would make Nikki Sixx smile. They don't think about their human rights – all are freaks together in the travelling-without-moving circus town.

Their Friends
Their friends are the dwarves and the Siamese twins and the snake men and the pinheads. It is beautiful to be deformed or crippled here – they welcome you with open arms. Babies are born, the circus town multiplies and multiplies, and we are all friends here. The runway lies ahead of them like a great false dawn. Their friend Zack is practising his cannon blast, whilst Louise cartwheels over the minds of resurrected deadheads in the audience tonight. And Strong Man Ned lifts the midgets way up onto both of his shoulders, singing as he does so – a Bertolt Brecht tune for the long-forgotten Weimar Republic. No one tells the rednecks in the audience about this. Simon the trapeze artist swears on his dead father's life he will never use safety wires.

When the show stops and the crowd leaves, they all sit around a campfire, trading childhood stories and then boasting of their intended future accomplishments. Zack will somersault with six turns in the air tomorrow night. Sammy will swallow an umbrella. Diego will sustain a human pyramid the size of one of the Egyptian ones. Louise will make a randomly chosen member of the audience disappear completely.

Hold Onto Now

Hold onto mental snapshots of now, because as our bodies get older, we won't be able to perform like this, and what once seemed like beauty will be conveyed as abuse. The drugs won't hide the deficiencies; we will not be elastic enough; we will not be dazzling enough for the younger cynical crowds sitting impatiently with their phones out.

All good things must come to an end. Does Billy have the judgement and strength to choose his moment and his exit strategy?

In an attempt to offer the ultimate performance, Billy and Marie are prepared to die amid the applause.

The Outline of a Human Body

Ten years later, crowds dwindle as the circus crosses the border into Missouri.

The bears have no claws now.

The tigers are muzzled.

The knife-thrower hurls at the outline of a human being only.

Billy is still alive but in the audience now, weeping for his dead darling sweet Marie every night.

The rest of the audience have no pride.

They do not understand the urgency of life.

Not to Be Taken Away

I have always enjoyed myself. Unhappy moments for me last about twenty minutes.

Paul McCartney is throwing a party in London tonight and I have been deliberating whether to go or not for a while. My girlfriend Annette wants to go and has been hassling me about it. She says that it will be the party of the year and that we need to go in order to get me into a better mood. I keep changing my mind on it. Paul and Linda are alright, but I was much closer to John and Ringo when I was living in Los Angeles. We all had our lost weekend period over there and we wore things down to the knuckle at times. You can do things and go to places with those guys that you couldn't with the London crowd. The most fun I can have in London these days is taking a group of people to a nice restaurant, secretly paying the owner after the meal (whilst going to the toilet) and then rushing everyone out to taxis and pretending to them all we are doing a runner. Only Annette knows what I am up to, and she has a good way of pretending along.

Our last album 'Who Are You' came out in August and has been selling well. It went to number two in the album charts in America and is guaranteed to be a million seller before the year is out. It is not a bad album, but I felt that my drumming on it was less inspired than before, and it all felt like a bit of an effort to be honest. We are planning a big American tour next year. I am happiest when I am on tour.

My anxiety about tonight's event stems from the fact that I am not really drinking at the moment. In the past I had agreed with Pete that however much we booze, there is really no way out. So, I have tried not drinking at all and am on a lot of anti-alcohol medication prescribed by my doctor. "We have a remedy, you'll appreciate," he said to me a while back. The problem is that if I spend the night sober, people will think I am boring and I too will get tired and bored quite easily. The middle-aged lifestyle isn't really for me, and I am not like Meher Baba and some of those other gurus; I do care what other people think of me, unfortunately. And the truth is that there is always pressure for me to live up to my wild man reputation and be Moon the Loon.

On top of the sky is a place where you go if you have done nothing wrong. And down in the ground is a place where you go if you have been a bad boy.

Should I go to Paul McCartney's party tonight or not?

I don't much want to stay in this flat on the 6th of September. It is Harry Nilsson's place, but it has an eerie feel to it. It is the very same flat that Mama Cass died in a few years ago.

I take a few pills and then I call up my man, and he arrives quickly and hands me some cocaine. I go into the bathroom and snort two big chunky lines, then I go back into the living room and put on my favourite Beach Boys record. A few songs in and we get to 'Don't Worry Baby', and the cocaine is really starting to hit me.

Annette enters the room, and we dance together for a while.

"OK, baby, come on then, let's go to this party."

"Yayy, I knew that you wanted to."

"Let's have a fun night."

"Oh, it's going to be groovy," she tells me. "Your friend Kenney Jones is going to be there and that nice man David Frost off the television and Paul and Linda obviously."

Annette doesn't really know about the cocaine. I have always tried to hide it from her. She can be quite naïve and innocent a lot of the time.

"It's the launch of the film, *The Buddy Holly Story*, tonight. I am just reminding you in case you forgot," she tells me.

I first met Annette in 1974. My marriage to Kim had ended and I was struggling to cope with the long periods when The Who weren't playing live. Back in the sixties and early seventies we were playing over a hundred shows a year, not to mention the festivals, television appearances and the radio sessions. We were always incredibly busy and getting ready for our next gig. Pete and I were into the 'auto-destruction as an art form' thing back then and our poor old manager Kit Lambert was having to constantly dig into our finances to replace broken equipment. We played the Monterey Pop Festival, Woodstock, the Isle of Wight Festival twice. We appeared on all the big television shows like *Ready Steady Go* and *Smothers Brothers* (when I blew up my drum kit at the end of the set and left Pete partially deaf for the rest of his life!).

John, The Ox, was of course my partner in crime when we threw television sets out of hotel windows, or drove cars into swimming pools, or partied with the best groupies around.

I think that was when I used to say that unhappy periods for me only lasted about twenty minutes.

However, when we reached the level of success where we were selling out football stadiums, that was when the touring became more sporadic and that meant long periods with nothing to do. I would try and spend some time with my daughter, but in truth I always needed a drink and I always needed to be around other drinkers. Oliver Reed, Ringo Starr, Harry Nilsson, these guys replaced The Ox and became my main associates.

I have been a bad father and a bad husband; I know that. I got married to Kim at nineteen and she was the trophy wife. Mandy is a sweetheart, but I never took her to school, and I never once went to a parents' evening. Not around enough, not nice to

Kim, drunk too often. Apologies mean nothing, though, when the damage is done. But I can't switch off my loving, in the same way that you just can't switch off the sun.

'You are forgiven. We are all forgiven.'

The party goes by without too much drama. I stop off in the bathroom for another line of cocaine around 9:30pm and I talk mainly to my friend Kenney Jones. I am very comfortable with him, and he is a fellow drummer who I can share a lot with. I tell him I am fairly clean these days, but at the start of the film screening, I secretly smuggle two glasses of champagne into the men's toilet and knock them back. It is OK; I have quit, and when you have quit you can always just have a drink. That is how it works, right?

But I feel tired quite early, and I haven't got the stamina for this whole film. So, I lean over to Annette, who has been talking for a while to Linda McCartney.

"Baby, I don't have the energy to stay any longer. We need to go."

Annette understands and we make our exit. I love her drama-free approach to life. When I first saw her in a nightclub in London, she was on a date with another guy. I chatted to the bouncer and paid him a tenner to throw the guy out. It worked a treat and within minutes Annette and I were drinking Dom Perignon champagne and laughing and getting to know each other. I have been thinking lately of proposing to her. I can't find any fault in her personality after four years. Each time I play a melody, it means the earth to my little girl. I must be onto a winner there, right?

We get back to the flat soon after midnight and I take a few more pills without Annette noticing. All of a sudden, I feel hungry again and I ask Annette to cook me up some lamb and potatoes that we have. Annette is undressing in the bedroom and as the food slows me down, I take a few more pills.

At this point the demons in my head are starting to rise to the surface.

I think about my solo album 'Two Sides of the Moon' and how no one bought it. I am nothing without Roger, Pete and John. But then I worry too that they can exist without me. I was the last member of the group to join and so I have always had that niggling insecurity that one day they might throw me out. After all, on the 'Quadrophenia' tour in 1973 in San Francisco, I collapsed over my drum kit after having been mistakenly given some horse tranquilisers. Did the guys stop the concert and focus on their drummer who might be about to die? No, they didn't – they asked if anyone in the audience could play drums and then invited some young kid from Iowa called Scott Halpin to sit in for me so that the band could finish the concert as planned. I never talked about it much afterwards, but the underlying message was clear – I was replaceable, and these guys could always kick me out at any moment.

Annette came into the room now and wanted us to go to sleep, but my mood had darkened, and I wanted to be alone.

"Can you give me the room? Can you close the door? Can you leave me for a while?"

I take some more pills.

Why can't we have eternal life and never die?

I think I am going to ask Annette to marry me tomorrow. I can get this right the second time around. I have learnt from my past mistakes. And as for the band, no more brandy in the recording studio, no more taking drugs before concerts. Keep on the straight and narrow, party at the right moments, be like John, be like The Ox.

Then the final demon rises up at me with hurtling velocity.

It is the 4th of January 1970. Tommy has been a worldwide smash and I am at the peak of my powers. Life could not be better.

I decide to accept an invitation for a discotheque opening at the Red Lion pub in Hatfield nearby. It all goes well, and we have a few drinks and then we get ready to drive home. However, a gang of skinheads out on the street have apparently taken offence at my fancy clothes and car. They start banging on the car windows and getting very aggressive. Neil Boland, my driver, steps outside of the car to try and calm things down so that we can get away safely. But this escalates the problem. With Neil still outside, the car starts moving on the hill because he has left the hand brake off. I jump into the driver's seat and try to take control of the situation. But I can't drive a car.

I am a filthy rich and pathetic rock star.

Down in the ground is a place where you go if you have been a bad boy.

The car starts moving faster and faster.

I try to steer as best I can.

The crowd of skinheads outside are reaching a frenzy.

Something feels very wrong.

I am a filthy rich, privileged and pathetic rock and roll drummer. I have no other talent. If I didn't play the drums, I wouldn't know what to do with myself.

I take some more pills.

Why can't we have eternal life and never die?

Neil was run over and then some of his clothing got caught up with parts of the underside of the car and he was dragged and dragged further and further.

Neil Boland, my chauffeur and bodyguard, was run over accidentally by the wheels of my Bentley that night. I was exonerated of any blame in court, but I have had to live with the guilt every year and my life has never really been the same since.

It is the biggest reason I drink so much. I need to dilute the guilt. The guilt is strongest when I am sober (and that is why eating this lamb right now isn't helping me). The guilt of that death leaves me temporarily when I am drunk.

The skinheads in Hatfield didn't like my mod clothing – my fault.

I never learnt how to drive a car – my fault.

I had definitely had more drinks than I should have done that night – my fault.

I cried a lot. I considered myself a murderer at times. I would wake up screaming. I suffer even without the jail sentence.

Anyway, it is late now. I am going to take a few more of these Heminevrin pills that my doctor has prescribed for me. Maybe they will help me find the real me.

Anyway, who says we can't have eternal life and never die? I am going to propose to Annette tomorrow evening. Tomorrow is going to be a good day.

Hunting Dean Moriarty in Manchester

'Your task is not to seek for love, but merely to seek and find all the barriers within yourself that you have built against it' – Rumi.

It was whilst I was drinking cheap cider in Sinclair's Oyster Bar that I first became aware of the rumour. The friendly barmaid Lizzy, who I had attended college with years ago, started telling one of her work colleagues, Laura, all about it.

"He was in here last night, you know."

"Who was?"

"Dean Moriarty, the great womaniser whom we all knew from college. He drank three pints in less than an hour and then left to invade the night."

Dean, I thought to myself, *we may meet finally after all these years*. And after the ultimate betrayal more than ten years ago. I need to show that I have forgiven him, befriend him again and let him in. And then, when I have softened him up and made him vulnerable, I can fuck him up properly the way he deserves. In the meantime, I need to behave like Mister Clean and keep my wits about me.

I started drinking daily in Sinclair's and roaming the nooks and crannies of the old pub. Weeks went by and no sign of him. I was out of work and living off the proceeds of a house sale I had negotiated the previous year. I was living up in Rochdale and commuting into Manchester Victoria every day. This pattern had repeated itself and repeated itself over the years. I sat alone in Manchester pubs often (The Egerton Arms, The Rovers Return, The Angel, The Crown and Kettle, The City Arms, The Millstone, Mother Macs) and stared into my pint and became angry at the injustices of the past and the strange serendipities and twists and turns of life.

After about six weeks of this latest daily routine, I overheard the next sighting. I eavesdropped on a conversation at the bar between two older gangsters. Their dialogue switched from the state of the government to a man whom they had recently struck a deal with. And I heard Dean's name and the details of a deal about to be made. He was going to be at The Unicorn pub tomorrow soon after dark to negotiate a crime that was going to be taking place in Salford the following week.

"We will sing him a lullaby."

"You can be the one to write a letter to his mum."

Dean Moriarty. I continued to hunt him as I always had. The man who symbolised desire, the man who taught me about lust and all of the other fast-paced sins. The man who had spent a third of his youth in jail, a third in the public library and a third in the pool hall. The man who, when he was a teenager, had engineered the biggest lie to leave me under police investigation, whilst he escaped to mainland Europe with a suitcase full of money. What a catalyst he had turned out to be.

Everything has a price to pay.

No bad deed will ever go unpunished on God's earth. Karma will creep its way out into the open eventually.

And so, on this crisp January afternoon, I left Sinclair's and walked past the printworks towards Shack and the English Lounge. I had my phone fully charged so that I could take some pictures of Dean and his associates. He may not recognise me at first, so my plan of attack was undecided. I had fantasised about this confrontational moment for over a decade.

Reality is so hard.

Reality is so hard.

Reality is so hard.

The money in my bank account was dwindling and I would have to get a job again soon. The night was cold, and I felt the terror that my life was leading up to a crescendo moment outside The Unicorn pub on the edge of Manchester's Northern Quarter.

A homeless man tries to accost me about one hundred metres from my destination.

"Have you got any change?"

"Sorry, mate."

I give him eye contact, but he won't leave me alone. Perhaps I should have brought Lizzy with me.

I think I can see Dean's body shape outside the pub in the gloaming, but I can't be certain.

Meanwhile, the middle-aged homeless man won't leave me alone.

"I need some more money to get a hit later today. Can you help me, pal? It is tough sleeping out here on the streets, particularly in the winter when the temperatures dip below zero."

There is no one outside the pub now, and I must be about twenty metres from the entrance. I let the homeless man keep talking. He looks awful. A rusty yellow beard and a face that is blotchy and jaundiced in places. I start to realise that I should probably help him. I decide to stand still and reach into my pockets. We make conversation for a few minutes.

"How did you end up in this situation?"

"I had an alcoholic father and I needed to get away, so I joined the army and went to Afghanistan soon after leaving school. I saw friends and enemies die and I spent time living in the vast Sahara Desert. I was wounded by a checkpoint guard in my last month there. He caught me out lying to him about some silk rugs that I was trying to smuggle at the time. I was held captive for a few weeks and made to wear ankle bells, a woman's costume, lipstick and henna all over my body. I was made to dance for some of the guards before I took relentless beatings and was abused sexually."

I realised as the homeless man was speaking that his facial hair was covering most of his features. In the darkness it was hard to distinguish what he really looked like. He did have piercing blue eyes and the air of an excitable madman about him, and this kept me slightly on edge through all of the conversation.

"I came out of the army about five years ago. There was no help for me at the time. My mum died a few months after this, and I had nowhere to live really. I had no structure and I had nothing to get out of bed for in the morning. I ended up injecting with another friend in the same situation. Do you ever struggle to get out of bed in the morning?"

I told him that I did and that it was getting worse every day for me too. *Soon I might end up like this*, I thought, but I didn't articulate this.

Eventually, I gave this man a tenner but then asked if he would leave me to stand outside The Unicorn by myself.

"The future is yours, my friend. And I wish you better than what has gone before."

The man smiled and thanked me and shook my hand. We shared a mutual moment of trust and belonging and then he walked away in the direction of Piccadilly Gardens. He and I were both loners. He and I were both tragic figures at this point.

I stood in silence now outside the pub.

I was wearing Doc Martens. I had been going to the gym every day since Halloween. I had my braces on and I had shaved my head the day before. I hadn't fought anyone in years. I let out my aggression on those weights or by dancing around my kitchen to The Beat and The Selecter. Now it was my time to be the 'Three Minute Hero'.

Power is still measured by money and muscle.

Dean, where are you?

Dean, where are you?

I walk around the pub and chat to the two bar girls a little. I order a Guinness and I study the historic football photos on the wall. Various people come and go, but none of them are Dean. I stay in the pub for over three hours and get so morose that I eventually walk back through the cold darkness to Victoria train station.

The next day I return again to Sinclair's and talk to Lizzy at the bar.

"Did you find him then?"

"No – I am doomed."

"He hasn't been in here since – just keep on looking, I guess. From what you have told me about his past he won't be going by his birth name. Just keep your eyes peeled."

Months and months went by.

Spring became summer.

Summer became autumn.

Autumn became winter again.

I took a job working as a bouncer and security man in Rochdale and stopped coming into Manchester. I never found the man who had robbed me of my youth and had ruined over a decade of my life.

I continued to have counselling and eventually, by the time I had reached my forties, I knew I was able to move on.

I created a funeral pyre out of everything that existed in my teenage years. The lies and the deceit. The arrest and the bail period and the trial. Anything connected to that period was thrown onto the huge funeral pyre that I created in my garden.

I decided to move to a new city too, for a totally fresh start. I wanted to go where the streets weren't paved with bad memories. I wanted to go where fear didn't linger in my head.

I knew that I worked in security as a reaction against what had happened to me in my teenage years. Like an honour thing, I guess, and as a big fuck you to what Dean had done to me. And so, I switched careers in my early forties and trained to be a carpenter. Now I could create things and now I could avoid the apocalypse. From my first day in this new trade, I started to feel that warm happiness I had remembered from being a boy and watching *Grandstand* and *The A-Team* on a Saturday, before my mum called me into the kitchen for tea.

Now I was ready to start again.

S
T
A
R
T

A
G
A
I
N

Dean had been bound to movement and the road. I had tried to follow that philosophy with disastrous consequences. Dean only paid attention to the present moment and the excitement you could get from it – the pure ecstasy and pleasure of that exact moment, whether it came from drugs, music or sex. To become happy, I needed to understand and embrace the past, the present and the future. I could do this in my new city with my new career and I felt ready. Finally, I am ready to open myself up and find love again.

TODAY

IS

THE

FIRST

DAY

OF

THE

REST

O
F

M
Y

L
I
F
E

Two of Us

They had matched on Tinder a few weeks ago. They had both tried other dating apps, but the simplicity of Tinder was something they both fell back on. Keep it simple: swipe right for a like and swipe left otherwise. Who wanted to read a load of self-obsessed garbage before even having a conversation with someone? A simple head shot photo with an age and a location was good enough for both of these two. They had exchanged a few pleasantries and agreed to meet at a bar in the Northern Quarter at 8pm on a Wednesday. Just off Stevenson Square and surrounded by dazzling street art that contrasted brilliantly with the damp and grey air, the damp and grey buildings and the damp and grey mood.

Henri arrived first and ordered a beer. Mary was ten minutes late but had sent an apologising text in advance. The bar was quiet, with only a handful of other customers, as Mary ordered a vodka and tonic from the young waitress with blue streaks in her hair. She instantly pulled her chair up close to the table and stared directly into Henri's eyes. Henri was initially unnerved as he hadn't had that kind of direct approach from a woman that he wasn't paying before.

"So, how long have you been single for?" she asked.

"Always. I have always been single. Even though I am now in my thirties."

"The thirties are your prime years, right?"

"Supposed to be," muttered Henri with a wave of sadness washing over him. "How have they been for you?"

"You are cheeky. I am still in my twenties. I haven't had the life experience of a distinguished man like you. I can tell you that my twenties have been rocky though – a lot of highs and lows.

Anyway, let's not get into that straight away. You are a painter, or so you told me in a message a few days ago."

"That's right, but before we talk about that, you are probably wondering why I am so short. I am only five foot tall. My Tinder profile didn't tell you that, did it? I feel like we need to address that in conversation before we talk about anything else. Also, it ties into why I am a painter."

"Tell me everything."

Mary was leaning forward and giving Henri more very direct eye contact. It was causing him to blush through shyness. She had warmed to this strange and short man straight away and her empathy knew no boundaries.

"Well, I broke both of my legs during my teenage years, and I am also from an aristocratic family that has had a lot of inbreeding. My parents are first cousins. Maybe not something someone should divulge on a first date, but I feel like you are a trustworthy person, and you are a person who isn't going to mock me like all the rest."

"Keep talking, Henri. I am all in."

"So anyway, the doctors don't fully know why, but I have developed the upper body of an adult man, whilst retaining the legs of a young boy. It is possibly something called pycnodysostosis…"

"That is a very unusual word." And Mary tried a few times to pronounce it. Together, they managed to say it on the fourth time around and they both let out a laugh. Mary grabbed Henri's hand at this point and squeezed it with both of hers.

"Well, if you like long and complicated medical terms, here are a few more for you. My condition could also be a variant disorder along the lines of osteoporosis, achondroplasia or osteogenesis imperfecta. Another doctor in the south of France told me it could be rickets aggravated by praecox virilism… Anyway, these are complicated words – the bottom line is I am a short arse and always will be. You have to find a way of dealing with the cards that life deals you. You have to roll with the punches and make the best of what life throws at you. I know these all sound like tired cliches to someone who maybe doesn't have to think about these things every day, but there is real truth in what I am telling you right now."

"I believe you, Henri, I really believe you. And I suppose these physical issues are why you threw yourself into being an artist?"

"That's right. I was consistently bullied at school and as a young man. I was mocked and jeered and laughed at for the way I looked. And I couldn't get involved with any sporting activities with my peers. I was slow, and I was physically weak, and I was hopeless at all sports. I ended up retreating into my own world and I found solace in art. Sitting and observing people and things and then drawing and painting them. I look for the things that other people miss. I look for vulnerability and tenderness in people. I try to bring to life characteristics that other people don't expect, in order to break up society's stereotypes and challenge the conventional establishment ideals of good and evil, of honour and sincerity."

At this point, Henri reached into his bag and took out some paintings that he had been working on in the previous weeks. Mary studied each one with care and commented intelligently and with pathos. The two of them sat immersed in the sketches and drawings for an hour, discussing matters of truth, artistic worth and sincerity. After an hour had passed, Henri realised that he knew little about Mary and so started asking her questions about her past.

"I was a troubled child, and I ran away from home at a young age. I felt like no one in my family understood me. I had a passionate yearning for youth and beauty, and I couldn't find it in my family or in the humdrum daily life of school and childhood friendship groups. I was drawn to rebel characters and to extremist art and politics. Before I ran away, my father had thought I was possessed by the devil because of the music I listened to and the books I read. He asked a local priest to come round and perform an exorcism on me. Naturally, I resisted, and it was the final straw that led me to running away from home. I still have contact with my family, but I keep that contact light, as I don't want to get sucked back into a life of conformity and small-mindedness. Once a rebel, always a rebel. And it is best to be a rebel."

Henri had never met anyone like Mary before. She was someone who spoke with total freedom and without judgement. For the first time in his life, he felt that he had met someone whom he could tell anything to, someone whom he could open up his heart to without a filter. And Mary felt the same about Henri; she had felt it from their first eye contact. As she continued talking, he ordered them both an absinthe.

"Have you ever loved?" Henri asked.

"Yes, but it wasn't romantic love – it was different."

"That is the purest form. The most selfless form of love, because you have nothing to gain from it."

"Yes! That is so true. Love that isn't romantic and isn't consummated physically is the greatest thing in the world. So long as it is mutual and not unrequited, and in my case it was."

Mary talked at length now about her life in her early twenties, becoming more animated by the effects of the absinthe, whilst still retaining her poise and the accuracy of her storytelling.

"The first time I ever saw him, he didn't notice me in the crowd, but I knew that he was the one. I knew straight away that I was destined to follow him until my death. It was like a youthquake moment for me, and I am still recovering from it now. I am damaged, Henri, but I need to keep on living."

"To keep rolling with the punches like me?" Henri quipped.

"Yes, I guess so."

"So, why was this man so special?"

"He spoke the truth. It was as simple as that. In desperate times of narcissistic leaders, cowardly men affected by reputation and money and tactical politicians with their thickly veiled lies, this man simply told the truth to me. The truth about how to live, the truth about how to love your fellow humans and the truth about how to survive on this earth if you are a rebel. No one else in the history books or in real life has ever connected with me like that."

"A hard act to follow. I am not going to try and compete."

They laughed simultaneously and squeezed each other's hands again.

"My family hated the relationship I had with this man when they heard about him. His other male friends and followers were jealous too of the connection between us. There were constantly people trying to deride me. There were made-up stories that I was a prostitute. There were made-up stories that I had come from a criminal and underground past. All untrue, but I guess people are scared of what they don't understand, and men feel threatened by strong women who don't conform to the stereotypes of a homemaker, a wife and a mother. I wasn't looking to upset anyone, I just stuck to my guns. Eventually, Peter learned to trust me – that was definitely a small victory."

"Did you get close to this man on a 'one-to-one' level, or did you always see him with crowds around? The closest I have got to another human being's soul was my relationship with Suzanne, but this broke down when she tried to kill herself."

"Yes and no. Most of the time there was a crowd. When he performed miracles, for example. I saw him drive evil spirits out of people. I saw him heal paralytics and blind men. I saw him walk on water and raise people from the dead."

And Mary talked in depth about several of the miracles. This topic occupied the conversation for more than an hour. Henri interjected occasionally with questions of clarification and detail, retaining his outcast nature as an observer of truth and beauty.

"Did all of this really happen?"

"Yes, I promise you it did, and I was there for all of it."

"To give a blind person back their sight would be a truly wonderful thing," Henri remarked with added passion. "I think I would kill myself if I was blind. I wouldn't be able to observe the world in the way I do, and I wouldn't be able to draw and paint with my own personality. The darkness a blind person has must be an insurmountable tragedy. I believe I would take my own life in those circumstances."

"I believe that I would too, but I also believe that helping and supporting blind people is one of the greatest things that a human being can do on this earth. It is not someone's fault that they are blind, just as it is not your fault that you have short legs. I can't perform miracles, but I can provide a lifetime of service to the disadvantaged and discriminated against. That is the goal for the rest of my life. That is what he taught me."

"These are beautiful words. I don't believe that my painting can inspire in this way, but hopefully it gives people pleasure the way that good books and good music do."

"I was never alone with him for long. He baptised me in the sea, and we had intimate conversations on two or three occasions when others were not around. These are special times that I will cherish forever. And I saw him when he rose from the dead. I was the only person who saw him on that occasion. Of course, people don't believe. It is hard to stay honest when there are no witnesses or alibis, but I have learnt in life that the most important thing is to be true to yourself. This is why I will not stay silent. The truth is that years will continue to pass since his death, and I am human and have insecurities just like you do, Henri. If you believe what I am telling you, will you keep regular company with me to give me strength in my long-term mission? Perhaps if we continue to meet like this once a month, then it will be good for both of us."

"It will. Yes, Mary, I believe you. And we will drink no more absinthe now. You are too good for that. I can go back to Montmartre and drink absinthe with all the bohemians and beatniks anytime I like, but I know in truth that it is really killing me. My time in the Moulin Rouge is dangerous and toxic. I am an alcoholic, and I drink to give me some hours of escape from the fact that I am a freak and that the majority of society will always mock me. Vincent is a better artist than me, less precocious but more naturally talented. Like you, he understands my world view, but I haven't seen him for some time now, and I know that he is troubled by great demons too. You are the first lady who I know will not judge me cruelly. I too would like to continue meeting once a month in this way."

"Can I meet with Vincent too one day?"

"I will try to arrange this, but his whereabouts at the moment are unknown to me. The last time I saw him I painted his portrait. Sadly, I haven't seen him since."

"At least you have some kind of kindred spirit there. I have no one like that. As a woman who is single and with no children, I am not trusted by most of my contemporaries. Other women feel threatened by me. Men either want to sleep with me or they brand me a whore. I live alone and I won't succumb to society's expectations of me."

"I understand, and I feel that in myself and Vincent you will have allies. I will defend him as a friend whenever I can. I once challenged a man to a duel for insulting Vincent's talent. The man accepted, but then didn't show up at the time we arranged."

"You are a loyal friend."

At that comment the bell rang for last orders in the Stevenson Square bar. The two misfits finished off their drinks, collected their belongings and exited the bar together and emerged into the drizzle and rain that had hung over them throughout their groundbreaking conversation.

"I am returning tomorrow to Paris to paint in the brothels. I find an affinity between my condition and the moral penury of a prostitute. And I also enjoy the rare people in this world who aren't conceited. You and I both know that such people are few and far between these days."

"I understand. Paint as best as you can, my friend. And we will meet back again in one month then. Just the two of us?"

"Yes. You have my word. This same bar at 8pm in exactly four weeks' time. I will bring some of my best sketches to show you next time. I have some that I was working on last week, titled *Les Deux Amies*."

"Wonderful. I will look forward to it. And thank you for your counsel today. You have revitalised me and I am more determined than ever to provide service and support to the poor and disabled for the rest of my life now."

"You are a good woman, Mary."

They embraced and then walked in opposite directions away from Stevenson Square. Henri walked with the support of his cane. As he reached the junction with Newton Street he paused and twisted open the top of his hollowed-out cane. He took three large swigs of the alcohol inside it to warm him up and then continued on his long journey back to Paris and the wicked world of the Moulin Rouge.

Everybody's Happy Nowadays

'Whatever people say I am, that's what I am not' – Alan Sillitoe.

Suzanne, the black-haired girl in the coffee shop, was consumed with a persistent and dark depression. Wednesdays. The saddest day of the week. The midweek slump when all the urgency and excitement of a fresh start to the week had faded and you were confronted with the reality of the monotony and dullness of your life. Men had tried flirting with her all week, and she sighed as she made another latte for an office worker with a hipster beard and a northern accent.

"Excuse me, love, what is the Wi-Fi code?"

"Where are you from? You are not English originally, are you?"

She was tired of being asked about her olive skin or the multiple tattoos on her arm that she had got done in Paris as a teenager. She was named Suzanne, after the Leonard Cohen song, because of her father's love for his music.

She worked in this coffee shop particularly because it was independent, and she felt that the owners had similar life values to her. There were shelves of great books about music and musicians just to the side of the counter. Her favourite was a book called *Tombstone Blues*, which was an encyclopaedia of rock obituaries by a guy called Nick Talevski. She often dipped into it for ten minutes at the end of a shift, discovering new information about Sid Vicious or Jim Morrison or Kurt Cobain.

Suzanne had moved to Manchester soon after graduating from university in Paris. She had volunteered on a project in Costa Rica and met an aspiring Mancunian rock star there, who had swept her off her feet with his guitar playing and his braggadocio. She made the move in 2019 and fell in love with some of the aspects of the Manchester music scene and history. In particular, she listened to The Buzzcocks, who she had seen at a punk festival in France a few years earlier. She loved their melodies and the sense of fun in their short and sharp songs.

Everything was fine until the pandemic hit, but then long periods of lockdown had seriously affected her mental health. She needed a sense of purpose and something to get out of bed for in the morning. She started lying in bed later and later in the mornings and putting less effort into her appearance. Wasted days followed wasted days and the relationship with her boyfriend gradually broke down. She had no outlet and no escape from him, other than the coffee shop, which was closed for long periods of the lockdowns. On furlough and experiencing deep depression, her attraction for her partner waned. She became suspicious of some of his reasons for leaving the house and eventually she gave in to the urge to look through his phone messages. She discovered that he was having an affair behind her back with a lady who had once been the road manager for one of his former bands. She confronted him about it, and he confessed all. There was then an awkward period when she had to stay living with the love rat until she got her life sorted. She was close to deciding to move back to Paris when the lockdown lifted, and the coffee shop opened again.

Suzanne poured her heart out to one of her co-workers, Elaine. Elaine suggested that she move into a spare room at her place in Hulme a week later. The rent was reasonable, and it seemed like a decent short-term solution, until she got her head together. And so here she was in the 'new normal', working five days a week in an independent coffee shop and feeling bitter and angry about men in general. Her mother had sent her some extra money in January and told her to try and move on by doing new things, having fresh experiences, meeting new people and going to as much live music as possible.

Live music fed Suzanne's soul and so she went to one gig a week to try to cheer herself up.

She saw The Buzzcocks at the Ritz.

She saw James Yorkston at Gullivers.

She saw The Libertines at Manchester Academy.

She saw Peter Hook and The Light at the Apollo.

She saw The Selecter at Gorilla.

She knew that she was drifting through her mid-twenties aimlessly. There was no desire to get married or have children and she also knew that her degree in Philosophy and English gave her little work opportunities, compared to her diligent school friends who were already carving out careers in Paris and London.

"What is Suzanne doing in Manchester? It is so cold and rainy there."

"Her ex-boyfriend was such an arsehole. She deserves to meet someone nice in the future."

Every evening, as she closed up the coffee shop after 5pm, she read a handful of new rock and roll obituaries. Arthur Alexander, who wrote songs that the Beatles and Rolling Stones covered. Marc Bolan, who died when his car crashed into a tree in London. Sid Vicious, who overdosed on heroin in New York City.

Each morning Suzanne played the song 'Everybody's Happy Nowadays' by The Buzzcocks in her Hulme flat, before going to work. It gave her the impetus to start each day with a positive feeling. And Elaine liked the song too, so it became like a rallying call for the two girls.

Things drifted on like this for some time. Suzanne was twenty-six years old and very conscious that many of her idols had died aged twenty-seven. She talked to Elaine about this a lot and they both romanticised their ages and their respective similarities to Amy Winehouse or Janis Joplin, in conversations between creating lattes and cappuccinos. Most of the clientele were young and the conversation seemed lost on them.

Back to that Wednesday though, that desultory Wednesday, when no one expected anything special to happen. Suzanne and Elaine had made it through the late morning rush and there was a noticeable lull when the red-haired man with a mixture of dark denim and khaki green clothes entered.

He ordered a latte nonchalantly off Suzanne and then picked up the copy of *Tombstone Blues* and started thumbing his way through the pages. This man loved skulking in coffee shops, and he loved the adrenaline rush of caffeine. Within twenty minutes, he ordered another coffee and asked Suzanne if he could place a copy of his recently published collection of short stories on the coffee shop's bookshelf.

"What is the book about?"

"Manchester, dead rock stars and how everybody's happy nowadays."

Suzanne smiled knowingly.

"You love The Buzzcocks too then?"

"I do indeed. And I think 'Another Music in a Different Kitchen' is the greatest punk debut album of all time. Better than the debuts of The Ramones, The Clash or The Sex Pistols."

"I think that too, and I saw them recently after the lockdown ended."

"When I finish my shift, why don't we go to the pub across the road and talk about it?"

"That is a great idea. I am working on my next book right now and maybe you can be a character in it…"

The red-haired man stayed in the coffee shop, writing his latest book on his laptop until closing time. Every so often in the afternoon, Suzanne and he exchanged bursts of conversation about music, about growing up in Paris, about Pere Lachaise cemetery or about the state of modern live music.

Suzanne felt that she may have met her next boyfriend that day, even though she didn't know his age or a great deal about his background. In the evening, as they drank in the underground Temple bar, their conversation flowed, and they both felt at ease and fascinated with each other.

They took turns picking songs on the jukebox. He picked some Captain Beefheart and some Velvet Underground; she picked 'Babylon's Burning' by The Ruts and a few Joy Division songs.

Around 9pm they both agreed that they were going to call it a night, but before leaving the bar, the man made a bold statement:

"This is my last month in Manchester. I am never going to live here again. I have spent most of my twenties and thirties here, but I have been offered a role at a university in America. The University of Texas at Austin, actually. I have decided I am moving there. Why don't you come with me? It's a great city."

"Wow, that sounds like a great opportunity. I have always wanted to go to Austin. South by Southwest music festival, Austin City Limits, I have read a lot about it."

"Yes, I have too. The Thirteenth Floor Elevators are from there, Nanci Griffith and Joe Ely. I am being sponsored onto a permanent EB3 visa that has just been approved. I have no direct family and am going there to be a lecturer in Native American history; it is the area I specialised in for my postgraduate degree initially, and then for much of my academic life since. I mean, I understand that you have only known me for about nine hours, but maybe you should be spontaneous. Joe Strummer decided to break up the 101ers and join The Clash in just one evening. How about you think about it for forty-eight hours and then I come back in on Friday and we talk about it some more?"

"Yes, OK, forty-eight hours to think about it sounds like a good plan."

Suzanne walked home to her Hulme apartment and talked to Elaine about it. She called her brother in Paris the next day to tell him that she was considering moving to Austin, Texas. She started reading all about the place online, the history of the city, the best bars and hang-outs, the top ten things to do in Austin etc.

Forty-eight hours is a good period of time to wrestle with an idea and by Friday lunchtime, she had made up her mind that she would travel on an ESTA visa to Austin and spend three months there. She had no idea if the red-headed man would become a lover or a close friend, but she wanted to be instinctual and say yes to things in life. So, she started off by saying yes to the idea in her head.

Suzanne played 'Everybody's Happy Nowadays' on repeat on her phone as she walked excitedly into work on the Friday morning. She served each customer with a joy and abandon that she hadn't felt since she was a child. She drank two coffees herself and was peaking with a caffeine buzz around lunchtime. She couldn't wait for her new friend to enter the coffee shop that afternoon so that they could carry on the conversation and plan the new adventure she was about to embark upon.

Suzanne was tired of being upset. She always wanted something that she could never get…

Please, Please, Please, Let Me Get What I Want

'What am I living for and what am I dying for are the same question' – Margaret Atwood.

Johnny had the day off work and was up early and prepared to fill the units of time with tasks and routines. Off the alcohol and feeling healthy, he longed for a day of adventure, something different from the day-to-day working life of a man in his early sixties. An escape was what he needed.

Johnny's morning trip to the betting shop perked him up. Racing at Gowran Park this afternoon, including the Galmoy Hurdle and the Thyestes Chase. The latter had been won by true greats of the sport like Arkle and Flyingbolt, and also the Grand National winners Hedgehunter and Numbersixvalverde. He placed a few ten-pound doubles and the anticipation of the races kept him sustained with energy until lunchtime.

In the old days it was going on tour that excited him and gave him the routine he needed. Back in the halcyon days of punk rock and even on the revival tours of the nineties and noughties, he had had the anticipation of a soundcheck to get him through the late morning and early afternoon. The roar of a crowd after a song finished, or the roar of the crowd as the horses came to the final fence with the result of the race in the balance. These were moments of life that couldn't be simulated. You had to feel the energy and excitement and let that flow through your own body. It kept you young and alive. You never really noticed the effects of these things as a young man, you took them for granted. You didn't know anything different. But as you got older and you realised that your life was finite, as friends and relatives died and as you had health problems yourself that made you realise you were not going to live forever, as these things all happened, you knew that you had to savour those 'roar-of-the-crowd moments' and sporting events and concerts.

And a punk rock concert was the best type of concert: it had spontaneity, short, sharp jolts of pure energy and a camaraderie with your fellow concert-goers that you couldn't get at a seated event.

And a day at the races was the best sporting drama: each fence could lead to a casualty and maybe even a death. The drama unfolded over five or six minutes and led to a nail-biting crescendo on many occasions. Then you could sit with your pint, read the form, make your own judgement, place your bet and build up to the next excitement. It was like sex with seven different climatic moments, each half an hour apart.

A curse on the Covid-19 pandemic. It had robbed Johnny of so many moments like this. Days spent alone in a house dwelling on a marriage break-up, acts of betrayal and a lifetime of various regrets. But now it was 2022 and hopefully there would be no more lockdowns. He was determined to savour every moment of the things that he had missed through the dark times of 2020 and 2021.

Walking out to the sandwich shop on Ryman Road at lunchtime, Johnny paid close attention to a road sweeper. The young man was sweeping with frank, confident strokes, putting joy into each one. His work was a pleasure to him but not so absorbing that he wasn't looking up at times and saying hello to the lonesome walkers-by. This young man was clearly expecting someone.

Johnny ate his coronation chicken sandwich at his usual table, whilst observing the passers-by and the road sweeper. Occasionally, he dipped into articles in the *Racing Post* or started humming The Stranglers melodies and lyrics. He recalled the tenderness of the love for his wife and the constant desire that used to go with it. It would manifest as a pain in the centre of his chest. Sadly, it was a sensation he had taken for granted, like the early punk rock gigs and the trips to the betting shop with his father. The reality was that his desire had dwindled over time, gone cold the way a cup of coffee did. Kisses started to be avoided and that is surely how we all measure love – in the mouth and the clash of teeth and tongues.

The revival tours tore them apart finally. She had moved on and he hadn't. He had never understood the concepts of growing up or moving on from the great times. He always wanted to behave like he was in his twenties. He did this in his thirties, in his forties, in his fifties…

Move on to what?

Grow up and turn into what? Everything you were rebelling against as a teenager. Had the Ramones taught you nothing?

The best gigs he had ever seen – the Ramones and the Flamin' Groovies at the Roundhouse in '76, The Clash at the Music Machine in '78, The Stranglers at the Brixton Academy in the early '80s – they had all involved the concept in Johnny's head that you vowed never to grow up, you vowed never to grow old. And the anti-establishment ideals and dedication to rock and roll hedonism had to stay with you until you died.

His marriage had broken up legally ten years ago (although it was dying for a long time before that). Gratitude and who knows how many other tangled sentiments had taken the place of passion. Indecency was replaced by respect. His wife eventually left him for a tax lawyer from Hertfordshire. They messaged each other on birthdays and at Christmas these days, that was all.

Johnny had lost track of the time and realised that the big race at Gowran Park was about to take place. He put his *Racing*

Post under his arm and jogged into the nearby Ladbrokes. The first leg of his double had won – a horse called Royal Kahala – and the money was rolling onto Longhouse Poet in the big race. He felt a private rush of excitement and anticipation as the horses lined up at the start of the race.

After some sketchy moments where the jockey had to display great skill, his horse galloped to a hard-fought victory. Johnny shouted his horse home loudly through the last two furlongs and then collected his winnings. More than three hundred pounds. It had been a good day off work, no matter what happened for the rest of the day now. He stayed watching a few more races and left around 4pm.

He walked out of the betting shop clenching his winnings in his right hand. At this moment, he saw the friendly young street sweeper taking off his jacket as he finished his work. A mixed-race girl with a beautiful smile walked towards him and embraced him. She was the one he had been looking for.

Johnny watched them together, smiling, kissing and walking away to the bus stop holding hands. He felt no envy or jealousy. He felt empathy and joy at what he was seeing before his eyes. This forgotten happiness was running around his brain and emanated through all of the old aches and pains in his body.

As the two young lovers boarded the bus and paid their fare, the rain started to come down and people around him started to open their umbrellas. All of the umbrellas opening broke the line of his gaze, but it didn't matter – he had seen the crucial moments of his day. The winter skies darkened, and the rain started to really pour down. Johnny didn't mind. He could walk the four minutes back to his house getting as wet as he liked. The evening lay ahead now, and he was going to listen to all of his favourite The Stranglers albums back to back:

'Rattus Norvegicus'.

'No More Heroes'.
'Black and White'.
'The Raven'.
'La Folie'.

And whilst doing this, he could finish reading the *Racing Post* and decide on his bets for the races at Huntingdon and Doncaster tomorrow.

As he put the first vinyl record on, Johnny's soul swooned slowly and he lay back on his sofa alone, alive for one more day.

Prospect Heights

We are gonna play you some of the greatest music to come out of Detroit today, ladies and gentlemen. Turn the radio up and fasten your seatbelt and let Smokey Robinson and The Miracles rule the airwaves with 'You've Really Got a Hold on Me'.

Martyna grew up in Prospect Heights in Brooklyn, and by the early sixties, she had a good job in Manhattan and a boyfriend she had met at work. It was the early sixties and the pill had become widely available across the big cities in America. For the first time, a girl in her early twenties could date a guy for a while without the constant pressure of getting pregnant or married. Of course, the older generations didn't really see it that way and applied the same pressure you would have expected ten years earlier.

Martyna's father was from an Irish family, who moved to New York City in the '20s. He had grown up in Brooklyn too but went to fight in the Second World War. He was killed at the Anzio bridgehead in 1944 as part of Operation Shingle – the combined British and American troops' effort of landing on the beaches of Anzio, Italy, with the goal of liberating Rome from German control. Martyna was only four when her father died. Martyna's mother was of African descent and had grown up in Atlanta, Georgia, in an era of Jim Crow laws and segregation. Her family had also moved to New York City in the early '20s in the hope of a better life. She knew little about her parents' courtship, but she was made aware by other family members that New York City was one of the only places where a mixed-race relationship like theirs would be able to happen.

Her job as a copy editor at a publishing house in midtown Manhattan gave her some financial freedom and independence, and she moved away from Prospect Heights to an apartment in Fort Greene, which she shared with a friend of a similar age that she had gone to school with.

After work, Martyna would often stay late in Manhattan and go to music concerts and dance clubs with her other friends, uptown. Berry Gordy's Motown label had exciting music exploding out of Harlem clubs and bars. She preferred being at venues that played this music and where the clientele was in the majority black. She was dating another mixed-race part-Irish guy who worked in her building, but it was casual for now. Dinner and staying at his once a week and no talk yet of anything more serious. This meant she had the freedom to dance with her female friends in her favourite bars in Harlem. Her favourite songs of the era:

'Please Mr. Postman' by The Marvelettes.

'My Guy' by Mary Wells.

'Where Did Our Love Go' by The Supremes.

'(Love Is Like A) Heat Wave' by Martha and the Vandellas.

'Every Beat of My Heart' by Gladys Knight & The Pips.

'Fingertips' by Little Stevie Wonder.

Times were good; the '60s were in full swing; and Martyna was loving her life.

And then, one April morning, two aspiring songwriters from California moved to New York to start writing for many of the big labels in the city. Leonard and Jerry were friends and co-wrote songs together. They had had a few minor chart hits but, inspired by that year's surge in record sales due to The Beatles' *Ed Sullivan* performances and the start of the British Invasion, they decided that they needed to raise their game and move to the Big Apple to network their music more and get songwriting inspiration from the legendary energy of the city.

To set the scene, here were a few key facts about each of them:

Leonard Archie Travers – born in San Diego into a white American family of Germanic descent. 185 centimetres tall, handsome and well built, looked a bit like Jack Kerouac. Dropped out of college and joined a few California bands. Obsessed with the surf boom and surf rock. Favourite album – The Beach Boys, 'Surfin' USA'. No longer plays in groups now and is focused purely on songwriting. Doesn't think much of the music on the Motown label. Has inherited racist tendencies from his family.

Jerry Samuel Phillips – also born into a white middle-class family in San Diego. Father had died in the first year of the Korean War. Leonard's songwriting partner. Shorter than Leonard. Less good-looking than Leonard. Nicer and generally more empathetic than Leonard. Writes home to his mother in Chula Vista every week. Favourite album – 'Crying' by Roy Orbison. Still a virgin, although he has never relayed this to Leonard, who prides himself on being a great womaniser.

The two friends rented an apartment in the East Village and set up various business meetings with the main record labels in the city. They had already written two top-forty hits, which gave them some good negotiating clout.

After a successful day of meetings at the Brill Building, Jerry suggested they went for some drinks in Harlem that evening to listen to some of the new sounds in the air.

"I don't know, Jerry, I am not really into all those race records, man. It might be a bit rough, and we might get beaten up."

"Come on, dude, this is what we moved to New York City for. You have to expand your horizons, Leonard. You can't spend your whole life reminiscing about 1963 and The Beach Boys. To be great songwriters, we need to expand our sound and take in more influences. Listen, I will buy the drinks, as this venture is my idea."

"OK, well if you are buying the drinks then fair enough. But I might head home early if I feel uncomfortable – I am just saying it now."

Jerry bundled his friend onto the subway, and they made their way up to 125th Street Station, just north of Columbia University. They found a bar nearby and had two beers each. Jerry then asked one of the bartenders where the best bars for Motown music could be found and he received directions (and a glowing review) to the Apache Club.

As the two young men entered the club, they realised they were the only white faces in there. Leonard became twitchy straight away, but Jerry felt at ease. They were playing Motown records, mixed in with some songs from the Chess, Atlantic and Stax labels. A few Ray Charles songs came on back to back, and Jerry was humming the melodies and enjoying himself.

As the last notes of 'What'd I Say' were being played, Martyna, the pearl of Prospect Heights, entered the bar with her friend Diana. They found a seat at a table right next to Leonard and Jerry and ordered a gin and tonic each.

Instantly, Leonard felt attracted to Martyna, and his eyes kept moving across to her during some of the conversation with Jerry.

"The music that John Lennon and Paul McCartney are writing has massive appeal across the races and across the generations. But their albums have a mixture of original numbers and covers. And all the covers are by American songwriters. If you listen to The Beatles' second album, it has 'Roll Over Beethoven' by Chuck Berry on it, 'You Really Got a Hold on Me' by Smokey Robinson, 'Money (That's What I Want)' by Berry Gordy and Janie Bradford, 'Long Tall Sally' by Little Richard and 'Please Mr. Postman'… dude, are you listening to what I am saying? We have to write like Black Americans; if we do that, we can start selling our songs on to all these English groups that are coming over here each week – The

Animals, Herman's Hermits, Freddie and the Dreamers. You hear me, these 'one hit wonder' British bands are going to need songwriters like us to sustain their careers. This is a very important time in musical history, and if we write the right songs, we could set ourselves up financially for life. What do you think about that?"

Leonard was half listening and half distracted by Martyna and Diana's conversation at the table next to him.

"Making a lot of money and setting ourselves up for life sounds good. But I don't know if I can write like a black man. How would I do that? I don't have those life experiences. I can't relate to their heritage."

"OK, so date a black girl. You are such a hit with the ladies, make your move on a girl up here tonight. Maybe that will give you the inspiration to write the songs we need to make us famous. I got some great lyrics right now, but I need better beat and better instrumentation to the stuff that we were recording over in California. We need some piano, and we need some saxophone, and we need to embrace the excitement of black dance music – that is what will make our songs really sell."

"OK, so date a black girl? I don't know what my parents would think about that. My dad and his side of the family are pretty racist, you know that, right?"

"Yeah, and that is why I had to get you away from California. Go on then, make a move on a girl tonight…"

Jerry stood up to go to the toilet and Leonard leaned across to the two girls and interrupted their conversation.

'Ladies, my name is Leonard – me and my friend would like to buy you both a drink. What do you reckon? I will try anything once."

There was an awkward silence.

"Well, hey, I told you my name, I think you had better tell me yours."

Diana spoke first and was a mixture of flirtatious and protective. Yet it was Martyna and Leonard who had the instant chemistry. By the time Jerry returned to the table, he was the passenger on this train. As the night wore on, he and Diana talked earnestly about the music industry, whilst Leonard and Martyna smooched into the corner and ended up kissing each other goodnight. The innocence between all four of them hung in the air that night. After all, it was 1964 and a lot of folks still felt innocent.

* * *

It's a red-hot day out there today, folks, temperatures in the nineties, and to match the heat on the street, here is a song for all you lovers, young and old. Written by the incredible Holland-Dozier-Holland songwriting team. Turn the sound up and dance the morning away to 'Heat Wave' by the wonderful Martha and the Vandellas.

A year later now and Leonard and Martyna had been lovers and been through a turbulent year. They were lying in bed together in a Prospect Heights apartment with the air conditioning on full blast on this sweltering August morning. Eleven months before, Martyna had broken things off with her previous boyfriend and, soon after, her and Diana had moved from their Fort Greene apartment to a slightly nicer place in Prospect Heights. Martyna, Diana, Leonard and Jerry had initially been on a few double dates, but when Diana had made it clear that she had no physical attraction to Jerry (by kissing another guy one night in front of him), the group split up and it was just Martyna and Leonard that continued dating. Soon after Christmas, Martyna came off the pill and became pregnant but had an early miscarriage. It was a month when Leonard was back in California seeing his family. She decided to never mention it to him as she didn't want him feeling burdened by it. She had confided in Diana, and Diana said she didn't approve of the fact that Leonard was showing little sensitivity or empathy for her best friend at that time. "You are only going out with him because he is so good-looking! I don't think he cares for you as much as you care for him! Or as much as he cares for himself, Martyna!"

Diana didn't feel comfortable in Leonard's presence and always tried to avoid him. She detected a racist streak in him and old-fashioned values that were linked to her ancestors' slave-owning families. Fiercely loyal to her best friend Martyna, she had tried to get this point across, but it fell on deaf ears.

Jerry too had distanced himself from Leonard. They had grown apart over the year and stopped writing songs together. Jerry was not interested in women at this time but began immersing himself in anti-Vietnam War sentiment and protests. He was hanging out most days in the live music bars on Bleecker Street in Greenwich Village and listening to Bob Dylan, Phil Ochs and Pete Seeger albums. Leonard found this all to be too pious and too sincere. He was still a frat boy at heart and hadn't really grown up. He mainly enjoyed a life of drinking, going to baseball games, making love to Martyna and sponging off the monthly allowance that his parents gave him.

On the 16th of August 1965, the two lovers lay in bed together in a morning pool of sweat. The night before, they had been to see The Beatles at Shea Stadium together.

Martyna had now decided that she loved The Beatles as much as all her favourite Motown artists. Leonard had bought the tickets, to keep her excited and so that he could brag about it to her friends for years to come.

In bed, Martyna had a pen and paper and was trying to write

down the songs they had heard in order the night before. Leonard didn't really care but acted along.

"OK, OK, I think I have got it right this time."

"OK, baby."

"You ready?"

"Yeah, hit me with it."

"So, I think it went like this:

"'Twist and Shout'.

"'She's a Woman'.

"'I Feel Fine'.

"'Dizzy Miss Lizzy'.

"'Ticket to Ride'.

"'Everybody's Trying to Be My Baby'.

"'Can't Buy Me Love'.

"'Baby's in Black'.

"'Act Naturally'.

"'A Hard Day's Night'.

"'Help'.

"'I'm Down.'"

"Yeah, I think you got it, baby. Ringo definitely sang 'Act Naturally'. I can't tell whether he is a good singer or not, but he definitely sung it from behind his drum kit."

"Paul is my favourite still," enthused Martyna, "but I loved all of them last night. Oh, we have to go see them again next time they come to New York."

"Well, you do tend to go for the good-looking guys. And yes, of course, baby, you can always rely on me to get tickets."

Martyna took a bath and then told Leonard she had to head out to buy her mother a birthday present. Leonard stayed in bed and fell back asleep until he was woken in the early afternoon by Diana, who was returning from a morning working at a café over in Bed-Stuy. Leonard was intimidated by Diana and didn't want to have to talk to her, so he dragged his clothes on and jumped out the window into the garden, to make his way back to his Manhattan apartment.

That evening, Martyna and Diana sat together in the kitchen with Martyna talking excitedly about the concert from the night before. Diana listened for some time and then the anger in her had built up to such a level that she exploded.

"You know in the café today I told my Italian boss that I wanted to see more representation of black people on the walls. He has all these framed pictures of famous white people like John F Kennedy, Marilyn Monroe, Humphrey Bogart, Babe Ruth, Joe Di Maggio, Frank Sinatra. But you know what, there ain't a picture of one black person on the wall, Martyna. And more than half of his customers are black. I told him it didn't feel right, that it was making me feel uncomfortable. Why can't we have some pictures of Louis Armstrong or Sammy Davis Jr. or Martin Luther King? But he didn't like what I was saying and at the end of the day, as I was getting ready to leave, he said to me, 'Diana, when you are walking back to your apartment in Prospect Heights, have a think about whether you want to keep working here. It's my café, and I am Italian, and I pick the photographs that go on the wall.'

"That was the last thing he said to me. I think I am going to leave the job, Martyna, and go and work somewhere else. I am so sick of the racism we experience every day. But I worry about you too – with your white boyfriend and you going to Beatles' concerts – I feel like you are out of touch with some of the things that black people are going through right now. Like I am in tune more and more with the Nation of Islam and the things that Malcolm X has been saying."

"I hear you, Diana, and I am on your side, of course. But you have to follow someone like Martin Luther King over Malcolm X. You have to believe in the power of pacifism. It makes the oppressor feel guilty and it makes them change. Violence won't do that. It will just cause more division. It's funny, I never talk about this stuff with Leonard. He says he thinks the Nation of Islam is dangerous and that Muhammad Ali is a fake world champion. I argued with him on the topic, but we ended up agreeing to not talk about it again."

"That's what I mean, Martyna. I want you to have a boyfriend who loves Muhammad Ali. I want you to have a boyfriend who speaks out openly against the Vietnam War. You are too good for Leonard, or he isn't good enough for you. There we go, I have said my piece."

Diana started crying at the kitchen table and Martyna hugged her and soothed her anger. "Leave that job then and make yourself happy – start something of your own, that has your own values and ideals to it. It is never too late to do the right thing…"

* * *

Good morning, all you beautiful people of New York City. We have music from the heavens for you today. It's another scorcher out there, so drink plenty of water, stay hydrated and let your soul out into the open for the wide world to see. And kicking things off we have Norman Whitfield and Barret Strong's 'Ball of Confusion (That's What the World Is Today)' performed by our very own brothers from Detroit, Michigan, The Temptations.

Five years had passed; Bobby Kennedy had got shot; man had landed on the moon; The Beatles had stopped touring and released 'Revolver', 'Sgt Pepper's Lonely Hearts Club Band', the 'White Album' and 'Abbey Road'. There was Monterey; there was Woodstock; Nixon was in the White House; the riots and protests in Paris, London and all across the USA, as the Vietnam war intensified. Tommie Smith and John Carlos had given black power salutes at the Mexico Olympics. Muhammad Ali was stripped of his titles and banned from boxing for three years for being a conscientious objector and saying 'I ain't got no quarrel with those Viet Cong'.

In those years, Martyna broke up with Leonard. She caught him cheating on her with a white woman from Long Island. He squealed like a rat as she threw all of his possessions out into the street when she kicked him out and she never heard from him again after that. By 1968, Leonard's allowance from his family had come to an end, and he decided to relocate to Carlsbad, California, where he took a job in real estate and married a local girl called Mary Lou. He still listened to The Beach Boys but by now had put on some weight and was living a monochrome nine-to-five existence, surrounded by Republican friends and family.

Jerry had had a rollercoaster five years and had now moved to Prospect Heights himself. He had completely lost contact with Leonard and was now working as a freelance music journalist for *Rolling Stone* and *Creem* magazines. He had been to Woodstock the year before and taken too much bad acid. By early 1970, he had recovered properly and had based himself in Europe for a period and covered tours by major acts of the time like Led Zeppelin, Black Sabbath, Deep Purple and Free. He was now Lester Bangs' understudy and making a good living. The reason he had moved to New York in his early twenties was now beginning to make sense, and he felt settled and happy.

On a hot August Saturday morning, he walked out onto Flatbush Avenue to go to his favourite doughnut shop and was browsing the different options when he recognised the two women standing next to him as Martyna and Diana. He had a far less preppy look than six years before, and with his long hair and beard, he wasn't sure if the two would recognise him.

"Hey, how are you two?"

"Jerry, oh my god, it's been ages, and you look so different. But hey, it's still you," remarked Martyna. She had always thought he was a sweet guy.

"Hey, Diana."

"Hey, Jerry, nice to see you."

The thought of Diana kissing the other guy in front of him years ago briefly crossed his mind, but it was fine – he was over it. Both the girls were looking really beautiful and had the style of the newly emerging blaxploitation actresses of the early '70s. Martyna could have easily passed for Pam Grier in *Foxy Brown*, with slightly lighter skin and a warmer smile, whilst Diana, still the pricklier and tougher of the two, could have passed for Marlene Clark in *Night of the Cobra Woman*. No recollection of the last time Diana had seen Jerry crossed her mind at any point.

"How have you been all these years?" asked Martyna. "It is a long time since we all met up at that bar in Harlem."

"I work as a freelance music writer now, and I live a few blocks away."

"Oh wow, so we are practically neighbours. You will have to come over to our place sometime… what are you writing?"

"So mainly album and concert reviews. I don't write music anymore; I just write about it. Writing about music is like dancing to architecture, right? So, I guess I just dance to architecture."

Martyna laughed like she understood him. Diana stayed plain-faced like she didn't.

Jerry reached for a magazine in his bag. "Here – here is a copy of *Rolling Stone* magazine that has my review of the third Led Zeppelin album in it. You can keep it."

"Oh thanks."

"So, how about you two? I know you are no longer with Leonard. I haven't seen him in years either; we grew apart."

"Yeah, let's not talk about that; he turned out to be a total arsehole and had been having an affair behind my back for a year. We still live together, and we both work for the Black Panther Party now – it's headquartered in Oakland – but Diana and I head up things on the east coast. I focus on fundraising and communications and Diana focuses on all our east coast campaigns."

"That's right," interjected Diana. "We monitor all police brutality cases and work closely with the NAACP and ACLU to campaign for changes in the law and to overturn wrongfully accused black brothers and sisters. We both report directly to Bobby Seale, if you know who he is."

"I think that's just awesome. Good for you, girls. I am really happy that you are making a difference and fighting for something. Those are the best and most rewarding jobs. The ones that really make your soul feel, right? I mean, the urban ghettoes and the unemployment and the type of discrimination that black people face, I obviously haven't experienced, but I know that just because a bunch of laws changed and MLK did his thing, it doesn't mean that there isn't still huge progress to be made in the world, right?"

Jerry had a bit of a hippy moment at this point, where he struggled to articulate his pure joy and admiration for the two ladies.

Diana felt fired up now. "You are absolutely right, Jerry. And you know what, police departments are nearly all white. In the Black Panthers' first year in Oakland, only sixteen out of 661 police officers were African American."

"And believe me, it is not much better on the east coast, Jerry," stated Martyna.

"Maybe I could write some stuff to help you. I know that John

Lennon and other big rock stars are very much behind what the Black Panthers are doing."

"That's an excellent idea," affirmed Martyna and started scribbling her number on a piece of paper she had in her bag.

"Here, give us a call some time. And come by and see us too. We both live in Prospect Heights."

"Prospect Heights, what a neighbourhood."

The three of them smiled and continued talking for five more minutes before ordering their doughnuts and parting ways. As Jerry was strolling back down Flatbush Avenue, Martyna ran back after him, grabbed him by the side of his shirt and kissed him passionately on the cheek. "Here, Jerry, take this and call me next week." She thrust a leaflet into his hand. "It is our ten-point action plan."

And she walked away from him like Pam Grier in *Foxy Brown*.

When Jerry returned to his apartment a few blocks away, he sat down in his living room amongst all the great vinyl albums of The Who and The Doors and Bob Dylan and read the leaflet fully:

We want freedom. We want power to determine the destiny of our Black community.

We want full employment of our people.

We want an end to the robbery by the capitalists of our Black community.

We want decent housing, fit for shelter of human beings.

We want education for our people that exposes the true nature of this decadent American society. We want education that teaches us our true history and our role in present-day society.

We want all Black men to be exempt from military service.

We want an immediate end to POLICE BRUTALITY and MURDER of Black people.

We want freedom for all Black men held in federal, state, county and city prisons and jails.

We want all Black people when brought to trial to be tried in court by a jury of their peer group or people from their Black communities, as defined by the Constitution of the United States.

We want land, bread, housing, education, clothing, justice and peace.

The likes of Jane Fonda, Leonard Bernstein, John Lennon and Jean Genet had supported these guys and, recently, J. Edgar Hoover described them as 'the greatest threat to the internal security of the country'.

Jerry knew that his trip to the doughnut shop that morning was going to spark in him a 'year zero' mentality, where he had to fasten his allegiance to a cause that had been gradually stirring inside him, throughout the growth of the counterculture. Now he was ready to be radical; now he was ready to step out of Lester Bangs' shadow and the other shadows that had been cast over his life. Now Jerry was ready for the biggest fight of his life. His brain was nourished and alive and gave him no signals of his past or of danger or future regrets.

Blackpool Girl

In Blackpool back in the 1980s, an Indian man named Asif, who had moved to England over two decades earlier, owned a small business that grew into a minimart. He also set up a takeaway business in the building across the street. Although he faced racist abuse every month, he was able to instil in his family and in his own being a sense of pride, hard work, integrity and toughness that meant, over time, the majority of his neighbours grew to like and respect him. He had a daughter named Gracie, who worked in both his businesses and achieved grade As in all of her GCSE exams. She was studying for her A levels now and had applied for a place at Manchester University to study law. It was far enough away that she could have her own life but close enough that she could come home and visit her parents in Blackpool regularly. She was an only child, and she was growing into an exceptionally beautiful young woman.

The biggest challenge Asif faced at this time was a group of racist skinheads that had been using intimidatory tactics to try to extort money out of him. They had also threatened to cause violence and damage to his business, unless he gave them a payment each month that equated to twenty per cent of his earnings. The leader of the gang, Nathan, had personally threatened Asif's wife with a knife and told her that harm would come to her and her daughter, unless her husband agreed to the deal. This particular gang had multiple successful deals set up with business owners all across Lancashire.

Nathan had been in the army and was in his thirties now. He had little in the way of career or job prospects. He was well built with lots of tattoos on his arms. He was intimidating physically and handled himself well in a fight. Since leaving the army, all of his income had come from intimidation and criminal activity of one sort or another. He had had a girlfriend at school, but she died of a drug overdose during his army years, whilst he was stationed in the Falklands. They were still technically together when she died, and the hurt tore at him and caused his violent temper to come out uncontrollably, especially if he had a few drinks. Nathan lived on his own in nearby Fleetwood and had become obsessed with the National Front and right-wing racist ideologies. It gave him the structure and purpose he needed in his life after his army years and his girlfriend's death. He was also highly persuasive and aggressively encouraged young white kids in the area, that similarly had little prospects in life, to join the cause he promoted.

Nathan had decided he was going to sleep with Asif's daughter Gracie. He had become obsessed with her when buying his regular takeaway meals on a Friday night in Blackpool. The obsession had grown over the course of two years. Nathan decided that he would let Asif off from making any payments to him in the future if he was able to sleep with Gracie. He told Asif this one evening as the takeaway was closing. Naturally, Asif was horrified at the thought of his beloved and cherished daughter having any physical contact at all with a racist thug, who was trying to bully and intimidate him and his wife.

One summer evening, Gracie was walking home near the seafront when the gang of skinheads grabbed hold of her and bundled her into the back of a car. They drove her to Fleetwood and held her hostage near the beach until Nathan arrived. She was terrified but also felt that she had a higher power on her side that would win through.

Eventually, a younger skinhead with a knife took her out to the seafront around 10pm. It was a June evening and still partly light. Nathan stood close to the sea on his own, wearing jeans and a hoodie. There was no one else in sight.

"You are Asif's daughter from Blackpool," he said quietly.

"That is right. What is happening here?"

Gracie had seen the knife that the other young man was carrying and knew not to do anything dramatic or sudden. Her calmness throughout the ordeal had gradually started to unnerve Nathan's foot soldiers.

"I think you are the most beautiful girl in England. I would like you to be my girlfriend. If you allow that, I will make sure that your family and the businesses they run receive ongoing protection from my gang, at no cost at all. That is the deal I will make you. What do you think?"

"I think we should let fate decide whether or not I become your girlfriend."

Gracie stared down at the pebbles on the beach around them.

"Here is what you should do. You put two pebbles into my bag, a black one and a white one. With my eyes closed, I then reach into the bag and grab one of the pebbles. If I pull out the white one, you win, and I become your girlfriend, and you promise never to take money from my family in a criminal way. If I pull out the black one, I don't become your girlfriend and you also promise never to take money from my family in a criminal way. My main goal here is to protect my family. You have a fifty-fifty chance of me becoming your girlfriend, and I will be totally committed to the end result of the deal."

Gracie's beauty and calm eye contact with Nathan seemed to hypnotise him for a while, and he didn't speak. His accomplice looked confused and gave Nathan angry glances. The other lads stayed in the car so that it didn't look to any potential passers-by that there was anything untoward going on.

"OK, you have a deal."

"OK then, pick your stones."

At this point, the younger skinhead attempted to blindfold Gracie with his bandana, whilst Nathan rummaged around the different pebbles near his feet. He took Gracie's bag and eventually placed two pebbles into it. However, Gracie could see vaguely out of her left eye, as the folds of the bandana left her with part of her vision, and she noticed that both of the pebbles that Nathan placed in her bag were white pebbles.

Her mind went into overdrive, and she knelt down on the ground in front of her and started praying loudly in a voice and a language that the two men could not comprehend. Her words were extremely loud, and her hand and body gestures symbolised strength and passion. The two men looked at each other and were intimidated by Gracie's actions. After a minute of her prayers, she stood up again and declared, "I am ready."

In her mind, at this point her options appeared to be bleak. She could take both pebbles out of the bag and expose Nathan's cheating, but she feared then that this might lead him into a rage. She could just refuse to pick a pebble, or she could pick one and have to commit then to being his girlfriend.

Calmly, she placed her hand in the bag and rummaged between the pebbles whilst chanting again in a frighteningly loud voice. She picked one pebble and clenched her entire hand around it. She withdrew her hand from the bag and, before opening her palm out, she accidentally dropped the pebble onto the ground next to her, which was covered with multiple black and white pebbles.

"Oh damn, I felt flustered, and I felt like I was being moved by a higher power. I am sorry – that nearly messed up the game. But you know what, it is OK, Nathan, you can just pick out the other pebble yourself and, from its colour, we are guaranteed to know which colour mine was. OK, let's do that."

Nathan stared at Gracie. Gracie burst his confidence and swagger with her calm and powerful eyes. Slowly, Nathan pulled out a white pebble from Gracie's bag and Gracie let out a scream to the sky above her. Both men stood still and dumbstruck, and Gracie walked serenely along the beachfront to the nearby bus stop in Fleetwood. She boarded the next bus back to Blackpool to see her parents and stayed focused on her bright future.

This book is printed on paper from sustainable sources managed under the Forest Stewardship Council (FSC) scheme.

It has been printed in the UK to reduce transportation miles and their impact upon the environment.

For every new title that Matador publishes, we plant a tree to offset CO_2, partnering with the More Trees scheme.

For more about how Matador offsets its environmental impact, see www.troubador.co.uk/about/